Sink or Swim, Vol. 1

By

Megan Reiffenberger

Dedicated to my family, who has helped me immensely throughout this entire journey.

Special thanks to those who read multiple drafts and offered feedback. Including:

Dan Reiffenberger
Sarah Reiffenberger
Natasha Ronke
Emily Berg

Chapter One

Brody

"Great job tonight, guys!" Coach Tanner clapped as my teammate, Landon, and I clung to the side of the pool, still trying to catch our breath. "That was a tough set, and I loved seeing the effort you put into it. For that, I'm ending practice early tonight."

I shot a glance at the clock across the pool deck. It was almost a quarter after eight. "Letting us out a whole fifteen minutes early, eh Coach? How generous," I grumbled.

"Plenty of time for another set if you're not careful." He tried to sound serious, but he was struggling to hold back a smile.

"I'm good." I shook my head and pulled myself out of the water.

He started laughing. "That's what I thought." He turned his back to us and started erasing the workout he had written on his marker board.

Coach Tanner was one of the best coaches American Swimming had to offer, and I was damn lucky to have him in my life. He whipped me into the best shape I've ever been in, and I owed a lot of the success in my career to him. As a professional athlete, I truly believed I wouldn't have gotten as far as I had if it weren't for my teammates and my coach. Swimming may be an individual sport, but it takes a village to make it very far.

Not only was Coach Tanner an excellent coach, but he had become like family to me. I was twenty when I met him and had just started living on my own. He took me under his wing right away, and helped keep me out of trouble. I had turned into a bit of hellion towards the end of high school, so it was good I had someone like him around to keep my head on straight.

"Brody, is it okay if I stay at your place tonight?" Landon asked after he had gotten out of the pool. "My dad is having people over, and you know how he gets. I don't want to be anywhere near there."

I nodded. "Yeah, that's fine—"

The side door of the pool swung open and stole my attention as I watched two figures walk into the building.

"Tanner, I was afraid I was going to miss you," a tall, dark-haired man yelled across the room. He was followed by a petite, blonde woman whose heels clicked along the pool deck as she walked.

"Roman, it's great to see you." Coach Tanner shook the man's hand when he reached him. "Camila, it's lovely to see you as well." He gave her a slight head nod.

Roman Howard was the CEO and founder of Howard Enterprises, a cybersecurity powerhouse that provided services for nearly 75% of the healthcare industry in the United States. He was also one of American Swimming's highest valued sponsors, and he insisted on making frequent visits to various teams to ensure his money was being put to good use. His assistant, Camila Hale, would usually accompany him, as she did tonight.

"You wouldn't believe the day we've had at the office," Roman chuckled. "And then, to top it off, Camila here scheduled a late suit fitting, which took much longer than I anticipated." He took a handkerchief out of his jacket pocket and wiped his brow.

"I was just trying to help you, dear." Camila wrapped her arms around him and gave him a soft kiss on the cheek.

"I know, I know. I do appreciate it." He kissed her back.

With a disgusted look, I made my way past them to grab my towel out of my duffel bag.

I didn't particularly enjoy Roman's visits, and that was only one example why. Roman, who was pushing fifty, was dating his twenty-nine-year-old assistant, and they flaunted it for everyone to see. They've been together about six months now, and it still clearly made Coach uncomfortable.

Coach Tanner cleared his throat. "I can see where that would be stressful for you, Roman."

A chuckle escaped my lips, but Coach shot me a look, and I tried coughing to cover it up.

"You alright, Brody?" Roman turned to me.

"Yes, sorry." I nodded. "Just a tickle." I had to turn away as another chuckle threatened to escape.

"Anyway," Roman continued. "I just *had* to make sure I got over here today to talk swimming logistics."

Shaking my head, I wrapped my towel around my neck, and started putting my kickboard, paddles, and fins back into my bag.

I couldn't deny that I was thankful for Roman's sponsorship. Without it, I wouldn't be able to compete as much as I did. But it annoyed me how much he insisted on getting involved, especially since he seemed to know very little about our sport. I was still convinced that when he was advised to sponsor an organization, he picked the first one he found. And now, after three years of sponsoring us, he still didn't seem to have a firm grasp on everything we did.

"Sounds great, let's chat for a bit," Coach Tanner said. He turned his attention to Landon and me. "Boys, I'll be out of town tomorrow, so no official practice. I still expect you to work out on your own. Let me know what you end up doing. Enjoy your weekend, and stay out of trouble." He winked at us, and then turned and walked away with Roman by his side.

"Hey Brody, long time no see," Camila purred as she walked up to Landon and me.

"And still too soon if you ask me." I rolled my eyes and continued packing my bag.

The fact that Roman and Camila flaunted their relationship in front of everyone wouldn't annoy me nearly as much if Camila wasn't my ex-girlfriend. It was clear she ramped up the PDA whenever I was around, as a way of trying to get to me.

Her mouth dropped open in mock surprise. "Why so bitter? Are you *still* not over the fact I'm dating Roman?"

"I've *been* over it, Camila. We broke up a long time ago. I don't want to be with someone who's only after my money, anyway."

She frowned and crossed her arms over her chest. "That was not why I was with you, Brody. God, when are you going to get over that?"

"You keep telling yourself that," I said. "Maybe you actually liked me in the beginning, but it didn't take long for that to change. Pretty soon, it was 'buy me this, I need money for that, and let's go on a really expensive vacation!' It wasn't hard to figure out you liked my paycheck a lot more than me. Roman will see it eventually as well."

"That is simply not true, Brody," she pouted. "I'm *so* sorry that I made you feel that way. You were always saying how you wished you could have all these experiences with your parents before they died. Does it make me a bad person for wanting to give that to you?"

7

I'll admit that she wasn't entirely wrong in that statement. My parents passed away five years ago in a car crash, and there were a lot of things I wished I could have experienced with them. But none of those experiences involved expensive shopping trips or monthly visits to the Hamptons.

"Oh, don't even pretend those trips were for my parents. You and I both know the trips were for you." I could feel my face flushing with anger. "None of those expensive items you wanted had anything to do with them, either. Don't you dare try to make it sound like you were doing something nice for me."

"You know what?" she barked. "If that's going to be your attitude about it, then fine. I'm glad we broke up. You treat everyone who gets close to you like shit. Your parents probably even went and got themselves killed on purpose just to avoid spending time with their ungrateful son."

Something in me snapped, and I lunged for her. Luckily—for Camila—Landon was still standing beside me, and he grabbed me by the arms to stop me.

"Brody, come on. Don't let her get to you," he said. "She's trying to piss you off. It's not worth giving her any more attention over it."

Taking a step back, I felt his grip fall from my arms. He was only seventeen—eight years my junior—but he was much calmer than I was in these kinds of situations. He knew about my history with Camila, and he also knew I often didn't speak or react before thinking about it. As much as it annoyed me sometimes, it was good to have him around in situations such as this.

"Now, Camila," Landon said pointedly. "Was there anything *work-related* you wanted to discuss with us? Otherwise, Brody and I will be going."

She shot me one last icy stare before she spoke. "Actually, there is something I wanted to tell you. I thought you would like to know that you're getting a new teammate. She's starting on Monday. That's what Roman and Tanner are off talking about now." She said this as if it were ground-breaking news we'd never heard before.

"We know," Landon said, unaffected. "Coach Tanner told us about her last week. It's some girl from Minnesota." He threw his bag and a towel over his shoulder to take to the locker room.

"Yes, a very *pretty* girl from Minnesota. Her name is Charlie. I came across her profile the other day while I was organizing some of Roman's paperwork. Would you like to know more about her? I have access to this information, you know. You could be the first to hear all the juicy news—well, first after Roman and myself of course."

I stifled a groan. The only reason they had access to any information regarding American Swimming was because Roman insisted on having a say in every decision that was made. Money really could buy power in this organization.

"Like I said earlier, Camila," Landon said, interrupting my thoughts. "We already knew we had a new teammate coming. And I'm sure Roman wouldn't be too thrilled about you throwing out company information."

She held a hand to her chest and snickered. "That's so cute that you're concerned. But don't worry what Roman thinks. I can pretty much do what I want. I do hold the same amount of power in American Swimming that he does, after all."

"Which isn't much, if we're being honest," I mumbled under my breath.

"Excuse me?" Her eyebrows shot up to her hairline. "You have something else you'd like to say to me, Brody?"

I shook my head and started walking away from her towards the locker room.

"That's what I thought," she shouted after me. "Roman's going to be hearing about this, just so you know. So, I would watch what you say from now on. I'd hate to have to fire you."

Stopping in my tracks, I whipped around to face her once more. "*You* can't fire me," I said through gritted teeth. "*You* have no real power in this organization. *Roman* doesn't even have any real power in this organization. The only reason he has any at all is because we want his money."

"Brody, come on." Landon put his hand on my shoulder and attempted to pull me away again. "She's not worth it. Let's just go."

I shrugged out of his hold and stood my ground. I was prepared to start another argument, but Landon was right: it wasn't worth it.

"You're right," I spat. "This is a waste of time. Let's go."

Spinning on my heel, I followed Landon towards the men's locker room.

"Like I said, Brody, Roman will be hearing about this!" Camila called after us.

Ignoring her, I kept walking away. I was one of American Swimming's most decorated athletes. I'd like to see Roman try to get rid of me for hurting his girlfriend's feelings. She had nothing over me, and it was time she realized it.

******

"Oh, yes! Homerun!" I jumped up and yelled as the Miami Marlins took the lead. In my excitement, I accidentally knocked over the can of beer I had been drinking. "Shit, my drink!" I scrambled to pick it up before all of the liquid seeped out. Once it was back in my hand, I finished it off, and threw the can across the room to dispose of it.

"Holy shit, dude." Landon grimaced from the couch. "You're a pig. You should at least wipe up what you spilled."

"Look, Landon," I slurred, getting up to grab another drink. "I don't care if you stay at my house, but you're not going to tell me how to live. I'll clean it all up eventually."

"You said that last time." Landon rolled his eyes.

After grabbing what was going to be my fifth beer, I stood at the entrance to the living room and took a look around. The place *was* kind of messy. Beer and soda cans littered the floor, dirty dishes were piled high on the end tables, and the carpet was so stained, I couldn't remember what the original color was.

Shrugging, I sat back down on the couch. "Well, I'm not cleaning right now. I'm trying to loosen up, and if you were just planning to nag the whole night, you could have stayed home."

"If I wanted to be around a drunk idiot, then maybe I *should* have stayed home," Landon grumbled, referring to his father.

Landon's dad, Mr. Davis, was having a party tonight with some of his friends. Most of the time, things got pretty wild at these parties, and Landon didn't feel safe staying at his own house— hence the reason he was staying with me.

To be honest, Landon stayed with me more nights than he stayed at home, party or no party. Mr. Davis wasn't a gentle man, and he was easily set off if things didn't go his way. To add salt to the wound, Landon's mother passed away when he was little, and there was no one to look out for him. I told him he could stay with me whenever he wanted, no questions asked.

"I'm not drunk," I scoffed. I turned in my seat so I couldn't see him and continued to watch the final inning of the game.

I really didn't drink that often, but every now and again, I liked to unwind and enjoy a few cold ones. Especially with how pissed off I was after the whole situation with Camila earlier this evening. When she said it was a good thing my parents were dead, I wanted to beat her senseless. If Landon hadn't been there to stop me, I'm sure I would have. A few hours had passed since then, but I was still pretty upset.

My parents had been my whole world. I was an only child, and growing up, we did everything together. They always made sure I had everything I needed, and they sacrificed a lot of time and money to help me get where I am today. They knew how badly I wanted to make a career out of swimming, and they knew I had the potential to make that happen.

I wouldn't have made it this far without them. No matter what, they always made sure to get me to all of my meets, and that I always had the best training possible. They were my biggest supporters.

Unfortunately, they never got to see my dream come true. They died right before I went pro, and it wrecked me. It didn't seem fair. I came pretty close to giving up on swimming after the accident, but I couldn't disappoint my parents like that. Whether they were still here or not, a lot of hard work went into making this dream a reality. I couldn't give it up.

So, I kept swimming, focusing on little else. A few months later, Coach Tanner made me an offer, and the rest was history.

I downed the rest of my drink and smashed the can when it was empty. Suddenly, I didn't feel like sitting at home anymore. I needed to take my mind off my parents and what had happened earlier with Camila. It was time to get out and do something. I flipped off the TV—I was pretty confident the Marlins were going to win at this point anyway—and stood up to go to the kitchen where I had left my wallet and my keys.

"Let's get out of here for a bit," I said to Landon.

He groaned and pulled out his phone to check the time. "It's almost eleven o'clock, Brody."

"So? We don't have practice tomorrow morning, remember?"

"I'm seventeen, where can I go that would still be open right now?"

"I keep telling you, you should just get a fake ID."

He rolled his eyes and shot me a look. "Yeah, and risk ruining my swimming career? I don't think so."

"Fine, I'll call Chase. He's always down for a good time."

"Ugh, if Chase is involved, you can definitely count me out." Landon got up from the couch and made his way to the stairs. "I'm going to bed."

"You're gonna miss out!" I called after him as I dialed up Chase's number.

Chase Thompson was one of my oldest friends, and arguably the single person who's had the worst influence on my life. We met freshman year of high school, and every time I found myself in hot water, it usually involved Chase in some way or another.

For instance, right before graduation, we decided it would be a good idea to set fireworks off the roof of our school. Nothing bad happened, but we did get in quite a bit of trouble for trespassing. More recently, we tried to pick up a few ladies at a club, who we later found out were actually hookers. It was one big misunderstanding, but it didn't go over very well when the media caught wind that Brody Hayes, professional swimmer, was picking up prostitutes.

Coach Tanner kept warning me to stop hanging out with Chase, and I knew for the sake of my career, something had to change. However, Chase and I went way back, and ditching him now just didn't feel right.

About twenty minutes later, Chase texted me that he was sitting in my driveway. Grabbing my keys and my wallet, I turned off all the lights downstairs and walked outside. It was late, and even though the humidity from earlier had gone down significantly, it was still warm enough that it didn't take long for my skin to feel sticky.

That was Florida in July for you.

"What's up, man? I'm glad you called," Chase said when I plopped down in the passenger's seat. His long, brown hair was pulled into a "man bun" on the top of his head. I never understood the fashion trend, but at least it looked clean this time.

"Nothing's up," I shook my head. "That's why I called. I got a lot on my mind, and I needed a distraction. What are you wearing?"

He looked down as if he forgot what he had put on. "Oh, these?" He stuck his thumbs in the straps of the pair of suspenders he was wearing. He was also wearing a plain white dress shirt tucked into a pair of dark skinny jeans. "Ladies love hipsters, and I'm planning to get laid tonight."

"You look like my grandpa if he was like, sixty years younger."

"Dude, don't hate," he laughed as he put the car in reverse and pulled out of the driveway. "It cool if we go to that club over on Kings Street, again?"

"Hell no," I said. "That's where the hookers were. I just wanted to go to a sport's bar or something."

"Really? A sport's bar?" He shot me a sideways glance. "Come on, man, it's Friday night—"

"I said no, Chase. I have my career to worry about."

"Alright, fine. No club." He held his hands up briefly to signify surrender. "I know just the place, I'll take a shortcut." He turned on the next street. "Anyway, what's been on your mind?"

I replayed my conversation with Camila to him, and how I had been thinking about my parents all afternoon. My parents were still alive when I first met Chase, and he had known them well. They didn't particularly like Chase, but they tolerated him for my sake. He'd also been there during my relationship with Camila. He was supportive throughout the relationship, but even he could tell something was off about her.

"What a bitch," he said when I had finished talking. "I never liked her."

Frowning, I shook my head. "Weren't you the one who asked if you could have my sloppy seconds?"

He shrugged. "Just because she's psycho, doesn't mean she isn't hot."

I rubbed my temples with my fingertips. "Sometimes I wonder why I still hang out with you."

He busted out laughing. "You'd be pretty bored without me."

We sat in silence for a few minutes as Chase continued to drive us through a richer part of town. I briefly watched the towering houses as we drove, but quickly lost interest, and decided to scroll through my phone instead. Glancing through my Instagram direct messages, I was trying to find out if any of the girls who tried to hit me up were in this area. Maybe I'd try to meet someone tonight, too. It felt like forever since I'd been with anyone.

"Hey, speaking of the devil!" Chance broke the silence, forcing me to look up from my phone. "Does she live here?"

He slowed the car down and craned his neck to get a better look. In the dark, I could see a woman getting out of a black Audi sedan. She walked around the front of the vehicle and clicked the lock button on her key fob, causing the headlights to flash. In the light, I saw it was Camila. I clenched my jaw. Of course, she was driving an Audi now, no doubt paid for by her rich boyfriend.

Chase pulled the car over to the side of the road across from where Camila parked, and he watched as she walked up the long driveway towards one of the largest houses I had ever seen. Three stories tall, it towered over the other houses in the neighborhood. The outside of the building was completely void of any kind of color, which made it stand out in the dark. It had white marble siding, four white Roman pillars in the front, and white trimmings throughout.

"What are you stopping for?" I asked after a moment. "We're going to look like a couple of creeps."

"Shh." He held a finger up to silence me. "I have an idea." Leaving the keys in the ignition, he opened the door to his car and swiftly crossed the street.

Panic shot through my veins. *What the hell was he doing?*

Jerking my car door open, I got out and followed him. "Come on, Chase. Let's go. I don't want her to see me here."

He stopped walking when he had reached the end of Camila's driveway, and bent over to pick up a large rock that was a part of the landscaping.

A devilish grin spread wide on his lips. "Not after we get a little revenge."

"What the hell are you talking about?" I froze to my spot, unsure how to respond.

"No one messes with my best friend and gets away with it," Chase mumbled under his breath, probably more to himself than anything. He raised the rock high into the air above the Audi, and I suddenly realized what he was about to do.

"Chase, don't!" I screamed, but it was too late.

The rock landed hard on the front windshield of the vehicle, forcing Chase and me to cover our faces as glass flew in every

14

direction. The car alarm blasted through the silence of the neighborhood, and the flashing of the headlights could probably be seen a mile away.

"What the hell are you doing?" I shouted over the noise.

Ignoring me, Chase reached inside the Audi, grabbed the rock once more, and smashed it into the side of the car, hitting as many places as he could, as fast as he could.

"Chase, stop!" Wrapping one of my arms around his middle, I did my best to pull him away from the vehicle. My other arm was stretched out in front of me, trying to take the rock out of his hand.

"Let go!" He grunted between gritted teeth. He swung his arms in an attempt to fight me off, but I was stronger than him.

"What in the world is going on out here?" A male voice boomed from somewhere behind us.

Startled, Chase stopped fighting just as I had managed to snatch the rock out of his grasp. I turned to face the castle, now lit up by floodlights. Standing in the doorway was a shocked Camila, and a very angry-looking Roman.

"What have you done to my car?" Roman screamed, now storming towards us.

I turned back towards the Audi. "Now, look what—Chase! Where are you going?"

Chase had darted off towards his car, jumped in, and sped off into the night before I even had a chance to catch up to him.

What the hell!

"Chase!" I yelled, even though he couldn't hear me. Instinctively, I went to run after him, but a firm grasp pulled me back.

"Oh, no you don't!" Roman whipped me around to face him. "Brody?" He looked surprised to see that it was me. "What in the world are you doing? Explain yourself!"

"Roman, I—I'm sorry," I stammered. "I tried to stop him, I swear."

"Yet, you're the one I find holding this." He points to the rock that's still in my hand.

Shit.

I shook my head and tossed the rock to the ground. "No, I took it from my friend. He's the one who did this."

"From where I'm standing, it looks like your friend didn't want to be blamed for something *you* did." Roman rested his clenched fists on his hips, and his face was red with anger.

15

"Roman—"

He held up his hand to silence me. "I don't want to hear it, Brody." He then turned his attention to the Audi, and his face fell slightly. "Such a shame. You know how long it took me to find this model with all the bells and whistles I wanted? You better hope everything is functioning normally when it's repaired."

Letting out a frustrated sigh, I realized there was no convincing him it wasn't me. "I can pay for the damage," I offered. I wasn't nearly as rich as him, but I could still easily afford to have the vehicle put back together.

"No, I'm not worried about the money. I make enough to buy ten of these every day," Roman scoffed. "No, you're not going to get the easy way out. Get inside. I'm calling Tanner, and we'll decide whether I call the cops or not."

"Please don't bring Coach Tanner into this," I pleaded.

"You want me to go straight to the cops, instead?" He shot back, his eyes growing wide.

I shook my head.

"Didn't think so. Get inside. Camila, watch him while I make a quick call."

"You got it, baby," she called to him from the front door.

Defeated, I quietly made my way up the driveway. Chase and I would be having a serious conversation about this tomorrow. What the fuck was he thinking doing something like that and leaving me to take the blame?

"Didn't get enough of me today, huh, Brody?" Camila smirked when I reached the front door.

I pursed my lips and rolled my eyes, but otherwise said nothing.

"You can follow me." She opened the door wider and turned to enter the home.

Following her, my eyes bulged when I saw the inside of the castle was just as grand as the outside: every inch of it was bright white. In fact, it was so white, it was almost blinding. The walls were bare except for the golden light fixtures, and one life-sized portrait of Camila that hung directly across the foyer from where we stood. It would be the first thing anyone walking into Roman's home would see. There was a long, red rug that guided one into the house, and it was the only thing that muted the brightness of the white room.

Camila led me into a sitting room to the left of the entrance, and then motioned to one of the pale blue couches circled in the center of the room. The furniture in this room looked like it was more for show than for comfort. The cushions were stiff, and all the pieces looked old, almost like they belonged in an antique shop.

Taking a seat, I took a deep breath in an attempt to keep my wits about me. Clearly, this wasn't my fault, but Roman believed it was. Would Coach Tanner believe my word over his? Honestly, I wasn't sure. I was still on rather thin ice from the hooker incident, so it really could go either way.

"We'll just wait for Roman here," Camila said after a long moment of silence. She sat on the couch opposite mine with one leg crossed over the other.

After another painfully awkward period of silence, she reached forward and took a little bell off of the coffee table in front of her. "Penelope!" She called as she gave it a ring.

A petite woman, who had to have been in her mid-forties, came strolling into the room. She had her blonde hair in a low pony down her back, and was wearing a dress that matched the color of the furniture in this room.

"You called, madam?" she asked. She clasped her hands behind her back and patiently waited for instructions.

"Yes, Penelope. You would not *believe* how this evening has turned out," Camila whined, fanning her face with her hand. "I would really like a martini, please. Extra olives. You know how I like them. Do *not* let Susan anywhere near you while making it. You remember what happened last time? I told Roman she should stick to cleaning from now on."

"Of course, madam." Penelope tipped her head forward slightly, her face showing no change in emotion. "Would the gentleman like anything—?"

"*No*," Camila said so abruptly it made me jump in my seat.

Penelope still showed no emotions and wasn't even taken aback by Camila's outburst. She must be used to her demands by now. "I'll be right back with your martini." She turned and left the room, leaving me alone with Camila once more.

"So, Brody," she said, narrowing her eyes. "What happened out there? Did the jealousy finally make you snap?"

17

I ignored her question. "What were you doing driving his car, anyway? He didn't buy you your own?"

"Of course, he did," she scoffed. "My car is at the dealership. The touch screen for my radio is much too small. I'm getting a bigger one installed. It should have voice activation too, so that I don't have to get fingerprints all over the screen." She kicked off her golden sandals, swung both of her long legs up onto the couch, and laid back against the cushion as if just the thought of fingerprints on her radio was too much for her.

"I see Roman has a space large enough for your portrait," I said, pointing to the framed photo of Camila that could still be seen from where we sat.

She had the thing taken while we were together, and constantly told me to get a bigger house so we could hang it up. I told her to get a smaller portrait, but she didn't like that response.

"Yes, it's about time I find the proper location for it, isn't it?" Camila sat up on the couch once more and turned so she could admire the picture. "Roman wanted to go out and get one of us together, but I just hate the thought of this one going to waste in a dusty attic. Besides, now that I live here too, I wanted the final say in how we would decorate."

"You live here now?" I asked, not entirely surprised.

"Of course, Brody." She narrowed her eyes at me. "We had made plans to move in together, too. Remember?"

Before I had the chance to respond, Penelope was back with Camila's martini. She gingerly set the glass down on the coffee table in front of Camila and turned to leave, but stopped when Camila cleared her throat.

"Yes, ma'am?" Penelope said.

Camila reached out her hand in front of her. "I can't reach my drink from here."

Penelope didn't react right away, as if one of Camila's demands finally took her by surprise. She took a step forward, grabbed the drink, and placed it in Camila's grasp. "Will that be all?" she asked. Her hands were folded behind her back again, and her fists were clenched as if she was trying to remain calm.

Camila excused Penelope and took a sip from her drink. "Anyway. Where were we?" she asked me. "Oh yes, living together. We would have been happy, you know."

18

I shook my head. "You ruined that, Camila, and you know it."

She frowned and opened her mouth to respond, but before she could, the front door swung open and Roman came storming in, followed by a very confused Coach Tanner. I tried to sink into the couch, praying I could disappear and not be here anymore.

"Brody has a lot of explaining to do, Tanner!" Roman boomed as soon as he entered the room.

Coach Tanner stood in the room's entrance with his arms crossed and an intense glare on his face. He looked right at me. "Roman said there was an emergency. What happened?"

"He destroyed my new Audi!" Roman was still yelling, and he was now pacing the room as if he was too angry to sit still.

I cleared my throat. "Actually, Roman, I was trying to stop—"

"I need him to pay for what he's done!" Roman roared, ignoring me.

Coach Tanner was surprisingly calm. "I'm sure we can work something out, where he can pay you for the damages he's caused."

"No, I don't need his money." Roman stopped pacing. "I want him to learn a lesson. He can't get away with messing around with people he doesn't like. And I know he's had something out for me ever since I started dating Camila—"

"That's not true!" I shot to my feet, my fists clenched at my sides. "I don't know what she's telling you, Roman, but the only problem I have with Camila is that she won't get out of my life!"

"So, what was your reasoning behind destroying the Audi, if it wasn't due to a fit of jealousy?" Camila smirked.

"I'd be curious to know the reason as well, Brody," Coach Tanner said, giving me a look of disapproval. "I did get out of bed to rush over here, after all."

"It wasn't me!" I threw my hands up in frustration. "Chase and I were going to a bar, we saw Camila get out of her vehicle, and next thing I know Chase is out there smashing the shit out of it. I tried to stop him!"

"Chase is here?" Coach looked around the room.

"No, once Roman saw us, he hopped back in his car and sped off," I spat.

"How convenient." Coach Tanner's narrowed gaze landed on me once more.

19

"I swear, Coach, I'm not lying," I pleaded.

Roman let out a frustrated sigh. "I don't have time to point fingers and try to figure out who's telling the truth. Brody, I caught you with the rock in your hand. I don't know this Chase. For all I know, he could have been the one trying to stop *you*."

"But, that's not what—"

"Brody. I don't want to hear it," Roman grumbled. He finally plopped down onto the couch next to Camila, who immediately went to his side and put an arm around him, attempting to comfort him.

"Tanner, Brody needs to be punished," Camila said, tightening her grip around Roman's shoulders. "We will not stand for this."

Roman patted Camila's arm, and then gently pushed her to the side, seemingly too upset for her comfort.

Coach Tanner nodded. "I agree that he needs to be punished, Camila. What do you propose we do?"

She pretended to think about it for a moment. "I'd certainly be okay with him paying for the damages."

"No, I said I don't want his money," Roman barked. "That's the easy way out. He will come work for me."

"What?" Both Camila and I said at the same time.

"Yes, that's what he'll do. He'll come over every day in between his swim workouts and work for me. Cleaning, cooking, running errands. Whatever we need, he will help with until he has paid off the damages. Camila, you said you wanted more waiting staff around here, now you will."

"No, I don't want *him*," Camila whined. "I don't want him in our house, sweetie. Why can't we just have him pay us—?"

"My decision is final." He held up his hand to stop her. "Is that a suitable punishment, Tanner?"

Coach Tanner ignored the pleading look I gave him and gave Roman a nod.

"Then it's settled," Roman said. "You will start Monday. Tanner, I would like a copy of his workout schedule so I can plan accordingly. Now, if you don't mind, I'd really appreciate it if you went home. I'd like to get back to my evening."

"We'll get out of your hair, Roman," Coach Tanner motioned for me to follow him to the door. "I'll send you the workout schedule first thing tomorrow."

Without another word, I stood from the couch to follow him. We shuffled out in silence and piled into Coach's car so he could take me back to my house.

Neither of us said anything on the drive back. I thought about making another attempt at explaining myself, but I couldn't gauge how angry Coach Tanner was, so I opted for silence instead. It didn't take us long to get there, but instead of getting out of the car, I sat there for an extra minute.

"Coach, I wasn't lying," I finally said. "Do I really have to go through with this punishment?"

His face was cloaked in darkness, so I couldn't tell what his expression was. "Yes, you have to go through with the punishment."

"But, why—"

"Brody, I don't know if you did it or not, but given your track record, I can't confidently say I believe you," he snapped. "I've told you before to get your act together, and I told you to stop hanging out with Chase. He's nothing but trouble."

I sank into the seat. "He's my best friend, though."

"If he was really a friend, he wouldn't be constantly getting you into these kinds of situations. You're a good person, Brody. I know you're better than this."

I didn't respond. He was right about Chase, but I didn't want to admit it.

"If you want to keep swimming for *my* team, you'll do as I say," he said after a long moment of silence. "We'll talk about this more on Monday. I trust you can manage to stay out of trouble until then?"

Nodding, I exited the vehicle and made my way up to my front door. Once inside, I noticed all the lights were back on.

Landon was sitting on the couch again, and he turned towards me when I walked in. "You're back sooner than I thought you'd be."

I scoffed. "Yeah, well the night didn't go exactly as planned. Were you waiting up for me?"

He shrugged. "I just couldn't sleep. So, quiet night then?"

"Not exactly."

He got up and went for the stairs. "I don't think I want to know right now. You can tell me tomorrow. I'm going to bed for real this time."

21

"Goodnight, man."

Wandering into the kitchen, I slumped into a chair and cradled my head in my hands. As much as I hated to admit it, Coach Tanner was right: I needed to leave Chase behind. He was a good friend—or so I thought—but the easiest way to make sure I stayed out of trouble would be to stay away from him.

But first, we'd be having a chat about what the hell he was thinking tonight.

Chapter Two

Charlie

My alarm went off at five AM on Monday, and despite not being much of a morning person, I immediately shot out of bed without hitting the snooze button. Today was my first day as a professional swimmer, and I was so excited that I barely slept last night. Even with only a few hours of sleep, I felt wide awake and ready to take on the day.

Only a few short minutes after I was awake and getting ready, my cell phone started to vibrate. I smiled when I saw Coach Tanner's name flash across the screen and picked up on the second ring.

"Morning, Miss Charlie!" he said cheerfully when I answered. "Just wanted to make sure you remembered to get up this morning for your first day."

I laughed. "How could I forget?"

"We're ready to have you. Did everything go smoothly with the big move?" he asked, referring to my transition from small-town Minnesota to Jacksonville, Florida.

"As smooth as I could have asked for. My parents were a big help." I smiled at the thought of them.

They had gone back home to the farm yesterday, and I already missed them. I had grown used to living a few hours from home while I was in college, but had never been this far away from them before. Now, I was in a totally different state, and it wouldn't be as easy to make a trip home when I missed them. Even so, I was excited to experience what life was like outside of Minnesota.

"I'm glad to hear that," Coach Tanner said, bringing my attention back to the conversation. "Also, I know we've gone over this already, but I just want to remind you again in order to avoid any confusion. All of my swimmers have slightly varied workout schedules, but you will all be together at your first swim session this morning—I'm looking forward to introducing you to everyone. At 9:30, we all have a weight workout, and then I want you to swim at the early afternoon session every day—that starts at one. If we

23

need to change your schedule later on, we can, but this is where I want you to start."

"Sounds good to me, Coach."

After running through a few more minor details with Coach Tanner, I hung up the phone and was more eager than ever to get going. Even though I hadn't physically seen him since he recruited me four months ago, we communicated on a weekly basis so he could check in on my workout progress. Through these phone calls, I spent a lot of time getting to know him, and I already saw him as a close friend and mentor.

I went back to gathering my things, which didn't take me long. In my excitement, I had packed everything last night. I already had a bag full of towels, a couple different swimsuits and workout clothes, and some snacks for the day ahead. I was set and ready to go.

While preparing a pot of coffee, I made a mental reminder to start looking around Jacksonville this afternoon for future employment options. Despite kicking off a swimming career today, I also needed to find another job to help pay the bills. Not only could it be months before I earned a paycheck from swimming, I wasn't guaranteed endorsements or advertising deals. Those were reserved only for the best of the best, and I had a lot of work to do before that would ever be me. So, starting this afternoon, I would start looking for ways to put the management degree I earned at the University of Minnesota to use.

Filling my mug to the top with coffee, I grabbed my bag and a banana and headed out the door. It was roughly a fifteen-minute drive from my apartment, and with virtually no traffic this time of the morning, I arrived plenty early for my first practice.

I put the car in park and took a deep breath as I took a moment to collect my thoughts. This was it. This was the first day of my new life. I was finally going to live my dream—which was both exciting and completely terrifying. Downing the last of my coffee, I grabbed my things, and headed for the pool. Even though the sun was just starting to rise, it was already a hot morning, and I could feel the sweat dripping down my back as I walked inside.

The pool water is going to feel wonderful.

I spotted Coach Tanner as soon as I walked in. He stood by the edge of the pool wearing jeans and a blue t-shirt that said *American Swimming* on it in red letters. He looked like he hadn't changed a bit since the last time I saw him. The only difference was that his dark hair now showed a few more streaks of grey. Coach Tanner had also been a professional swimmer in his glory days, but now that he was in his late forties, he wasn't in the same shape he used to be. He wasn't overweight by any means, but he had certainly picked up a few pounds since he quit swimming regularly.

He looked up when I walked in the door, and his face lit up immediately as he waved me over to him. He was standing by a small group of swimmers who were doing various stretches on the side of the pool deck.

"Good to see you, Charlie." Coach Tanner wrapped me up in a side hug as I approached him. He was an incredibly sweet man, and even though I had just spoken to him on the phone less than an hour ago, I was already happy to talk to him again. "Are you ready to meet everyone?"

"I sure am." I grinned. Although I was excited, I was a bit nervous as well. Coach Tanner told me a few things about his other swimmers, and I had followed their stats closely over the last few months. His swimmers were the real deal. And while I knew that Coach Tanner wouldn't have signed me to his team if he didn't think I was fast enough, another part of me worried I wouldn't be able to live up to his expectations.

"Everyone, I need you to gather round me please," Coach Tanner called as he turned to the others. They stopped their stretches and turned their attention towards us. "This young lady here is the new recruit I was telling you about: Charlotte Price. She goes by Charlie, she's an excellent backstroker, and she just moved thousands of miles away from home. I expect all of you to welcome her into our little family with open arms."

I gave them a shy smile and a little wave. "Hello, I'm very excited to be here."

"I want to introduce everyone quickly before we get in the pool." Coach Tanner pointed to the only other female in the group. "This is Allison Benson, she's my star breaststroker. She's about your age, so I'm certain you will become good friends. She's a total sweetheart, one of the nicest young ladies I have ever had the privilege of coaching."

"Don't make me blush, Coach!" She walked over to me and shook my hand. "It's nice to meet you, Charlie. If you ever need anything, don't hesitate to ask."

I had heard of Allison before. I knew she had competed in the Olympics and held the American record in the 200 breaststroke. Standing next to her now, she was a lot taller than I thought she would be. She had to be well over six feet tall. Not only did she have a height advantage, but she was also completely jacked. Her arms were so muscular, she could probably snap me like a toothpick, and I could see a perfectly defined six-pack underneath her black TYR one-piece. I'd be lying if I said I didn't feel slightly intimidated by her.

"This here is Brody Hayes," Coach Tanner continued. "He's probably my most well-known swimmer right now since he took home two gold medals at the last Olympics, and three others at the World Championships," Coach Tanner bragged as he pointed in Brody's direction.

My gaze followed his finger, and my mouth nearly dropped to the floor. Like Allison, I had seen Brody on TV before—and in advertisements and magazines and what not—but nothing could have prepared me for how good-looking he was in person. He was the definition of tall, dark, and handsome. He was a little taller than Allison and had short dark brown hair. I took a quick glance up and down his beautifully toned body, soaking up all the details. My eyes lingered a little too long on his washboard abs, and the V shape that led to the top of his suit. I looked back at his face and the bluest eyes were staring right back.

Shit, he totally just caught me checking him out.

His mouth curled up into a smirk and he shook his head back and forth, clearly amused. I had a feeling he was used to women having this reaction to him, and I immediately felt annoyed with myself for feeding his ego. I was his teammate now, not some star-struck fan. I'd have to watch myself around this guy.

"And this here is Landon Davis." Coach Tanner snapped me back from my thoughts. "He moved to Jacksonville about a year ago, and has been with us ever since. He's our youngest teammate, only seventeen, and has one year left of high school, but boy is he quick."

I gave a little wave to Landon, who simply smiled at me as he said hello. He was definitely the smallest of the bunch, even shorter than myself. He had thick black hair, and dark eyes to match. He had muscles on him, but nothing like Allison or Brody, and he was very thin. Unlike the others, I didn't have a lot of information on Landon, so I really didn't know what his strengths were. But Coach did say he'd only been here a year. He was probably still trying to make a name for himself.

Coach Tanner clapped his hands together and went to the board to start writing the workout. "Allison, would you please show Charlie where she can change and get ready? I want everyone in the water in the next fifteen minutes." He turned his back to us and became absorbed with scribbling out our workout.

"Sure thing, Coach." Allison smiled at me and waved her arm directing me to follow her to the locker room. When we entered the room, she took me to a small section in the back and pointed to one of the larger lockers. "Here's the combination to your locker," she said, handing me a piece of paper. "Yours is this one, number twenty-two."

"Thanks," I said shyly as I worked to open it.

"How long have you been swimming?" she asked as she sat down on the bench across from mine.

"Almost eighteen years if you can believe it. I started when I was six."

"Time flies, doesn't it?" She chuckled. "I started around that age, too. Now here I am, twenty-four-years-old, and finally making mama proud!"

It was my turn to laugh. "Please, I'm sure you made her proud long before now."

She shrugged. "Probably. She always told me I would make it if I worked hard."

"My parents always said the same thing."

"Isn't it annoying when they're right?" She threw her hands up sarcastically and laughed again. "Anyway, if you don't mind me asking, is this the first time you've been recruited as a professional?"

Shaking my head, I finally got my locker door open. "I don't mind at all. I was actually recruited right out of high school, and got a couple of offers while I was in college, but I turned them all down.

27

My parents were supportive of my dream of becoming a professional athlete, but they also stressed the importance of a college education."

"Makes sense." She nodded. "So, you swam in school then, I'm assuming?"

"Yes, that was another reason I rejected the offers. If I had become a professional athlete right away, I wouldn't have been allowed to compete at the collegiate level, and that was something I didn't want to miss out on."

"I had to make that tough choice, too," Allison said. "Although, I did the opposite. I chose to go to school online and accepted a contract with Coach Tanner about a year out of high school. I haven't regretted it, I've loved every second of it, but a part of me wonders what it would have been like had I taken the collegiate path."

"It was amazing," I said as I started changing into my suit. "The friends I made, the places I've been. I don't think I'd change it for the world. But it was risky, too, delaying my professional career. I mean, how many swimmers do you know that first start at twenty-three? I think I got lucky, and I'm grateful Coach Tanner still sees potential in me."

"Girl, luck has nothing to do with it. If you're here, then you've earned it. Besides, it's not like twenty-three is *old*. I'm right there with you, and I can safely say we've got plenty of swimming years left in us."

I smiled. "You're probably right."

"I know I'm right." She returned my smile as she stood up from the bench and made her way to the door. "I'll let you get ready. Holler if you need anything, I'll be stretching on deck."

I was already starting to like Allison. Coach Tanner was awesome, and Landon seemed pretty chill. However, I was still a little uncertain about the other member of my team. Brody clearly knew the effect he had on the ladies, and I would have to make damn sure he didn't catch me checking him out again. The last thing I wanted was to give him the satisfaction of knowing I found him attractive. I wonder if Allison ever had any issues with him. Should I ask her? I shook my head. I didn't need to start any drama on my first day.

For now, I was already getting along well with two out of the four new people I would be spending all my time with, and that wasn't a bad start for the first day. Soon, I would get to know all of them much better, and our awkward introductions would be a thing of the past.

After all, it couldn't possibly get any worse than that.

Chapter Three

Brody

Camila had mentioned the other day the new girl would be pretty, but "pretty" was an understatement when it came to Charlie Price. As soon as she walked into the building, I couldn't take my eyes off her. She was stunning in every way possible. Her thick, wavy brown hair was pulled up in a messy ponytail, and her face carried no trace of makeup. Not that she needed it, she was beautiful without it. She was tall—not quite as tall as Allison, but few women were—and she was in fantastic shape. Her arms and legs were perfectly toned, and her ass was one of the best I had ever seen. I couldn't wait to see her when she had her swimsuit on.

She'd probably look even better with nothing on.

The thought made me smile. She was totally checking me out a minute ago, so she'd probably be down to have some fun. It would be risky, though. I'd never gone after a teammate before, and things could get messy if she wanted more than just a casual fling.

I shook my head. Hadn't I already done enough to risk ruining my career? It was time I started thinking with my head instead of my emotions—or other body parts for that matter.

Damn, she was hot though. She might be worth the risk.

"Brody, did you hear from Roman over the weekend?" Coach Tanner asked, snapping me back from my thoughts. "He wants you to start working for him this afternoon around three."

I nodded. "Alright." I picked up my equipment bag and walked to the side of the pool, pulling out my kickboard, paddles, and pull buoy so I would be ready for the practice.

"I think we need to talk about what happened Friday night." Coach Tanner appeared at my side once more. "I can't keep getting you out of trouble, Brody. If you have an issue with that woman—"

"I don't have an issue with her." I stretched my arms above my head, praying he would drop it and let me get ready. However, I saw him studying me out of the corner of my eye. I knew he wasn't going to let it go that easily.

"Brody. Look at me," he finally said.

I dropped my arms to my side with a loud smack and turned to face him. "I don't have anything else to tell you, Coach. I was telling you the truth the other day. I didn't do it. Chase did."

And he had conveniently stopped answering his phone ever since that night. If anything, Chase was definitely making it easier to not want to be his friend anymore.

"I just don't understand why Chase would do something like that." Coach shook his head. "I mean, I know he's reckless, but it doesn't make sense. Unless you asked him to do it?"

"Why would I ask him to do that?" I snapped. "You think I *want* to spend more time around that woman?"

He held up his palms in surrender. "Okay, okay. But just in case, I want you to know that you can do better. I don't know what all happened that night, but getting revenge isn't going to change whatever happened between you and Camila." He placed a hand on my shoulder. "And if you ever want to talk about it, I'm here to listen."

I stared at his hand on my shoulder for a moment and then brushed it off. "Thanks, Coach, but there's nothing to talk about. Can we get started?"

He gave a solemn nod. "Sure." He clapped his hands and motioned the others over. "Alright guys, time to get in the water. We have the whole pool, but I want you to split up into two lanes this morning. It'll be better to have someone push you. I want Allison and Brody in lane one, and Charlie and Landon in lane two."

To my surprise, I felt my heart sink a little when I didn't get put in Charlie's lane. I wanted a chance to talk to her in between sets and find out what she was like. What was her favorite stroke? What did she do outside of swimming? Where did she grow up—?

Wait a minute. I didn't think like this. If anything, I just wanted to find out if the look she gave me this morning meant what I thought it did. I shouldn't care—scratch that—I *don't* care about anything else. I didn't need to get to know her, I just wanted to have some fun. Otherwise, she was just some girl I was swimming with. Nothing more.

We hopped into our respective lanes one by one and started the warmup. I took it nice and easy at first, and then decided to stay even with Charlie for a while. As we swam, I watched her out of the corner of my eye. Her stroke was beautifully long and smooth, and it seemed as though she was going for a joy ride, even though I felt her picking up the pace with each lap. After a few more laps, I realized I was acting like a creep trying to stay in sync with her, and she was probably picking up the pace in an attempt to pull away from me. I backed off and went at my own pace for the rest of the warmup.

As hard as I tried, though, I couldn't *not* pay attention to her during the workout. I was curious to see how good of a swimmer she was, and I caught myself watching her more than once throughout the morning. When we started getting into the main sets, it was clear that she was a remarkable athlete. Her technique was flawless. She was so smooth, it appeared as though she was just gliding on top of the water. There was no doubt she was born with a natural talent for swimming.

It also became clear that Coach Tanner was right when he said she was an excellent backstroker. During the stroke sets, I was surprised at how well she was keeping up with me on the backstroke parts; she was even beating Allison and Landon. Backstroke was clearly her strength, but even as we did all the other strokes, it was hard to determine which was her weakest. She was phenomenal at all of them.

As the practice wore on, she breathed heavier and her face flushed red. She still kept up with all of us, but it was clear she was getting tired. At least this way I knew she was still human, and not some machine plowing her way through Coach Tanner's practice. I'd been swimming with him for almost five years, I knew his practices weren't easy, and I'd be lying if I said I wasn't impressed with how she was handling it so far. It'd be interesting to see how she performed this season.

As nine o'clock neared, Coach told us to do a long cool down before our 9:30 lifting session. Charlie grabbed her kickboard and began a slow, steady kick down the length of the pool to stretch her legs. Seeing this as an opportunity to make my move, I grabbed my board and kicked to catch up to her.

"How was that for your first practice as a professional swimmer?" I asked, pulling up beside her.

She jumped and looked surprised to see me. "It was good," she said, avoiding eye contact.

"I think you killed it. That was a tough practice."

"Are they usually like this, or was this a particularly difficult one?"

She continued to stare straight ahead even though I was mentally begging her to look my way. I slanted my kickboard towards her in order to swim closer to her. Eventually she would have to look at me.

"I'd say this was probably an average workout."

"Oh, wonderful!" she quipped. "I was sucking air by the end."

"You hid it well." I chuckled. "It's only the first one, it'll get easier. These first few weeks will be the hardest, though."

"Something to look forward to."

"I know I'm looking forward to it. I'm glad you're here with us." I gave her a sincere smile and playfully nudged her shoulder with my arm.

"Yeah, me too." She finally looked me in the eye, and the slightest hint of a smile appeared on her lips, but it disappeared as quickly as it came.

I waited for her to say something more, but she went back to staring at the water in front of her. We were now so close together our arms were nearly brushing up against each other. After another moment, it was clear she wasn't going to say anything else.

"You have a beautiful stroke, by the way," I said, trying to keep her talking. "Especially your backstroke."

"Thank you, it's my favorite," she said before she fell silent again.

Why was she making it so hard to talk to her? Was she shy or something? She was checking me out this morning—I saw it. Now, she was almost acting like she wanted nothing to do with me, and it bothered me.

Why did it bother me?

We finished the cool down in agonizing silence, and she pulled herself out of the water to gather her things to change for the lifting session. I watched her as she placed her equipment into her bag, then turned towards the locker room. The further she walked away, the more I felt like my opportunity was slipping away from me. I hauled myself out of the water with one jump, grabbed my towel, and went after her.

"Hey, Charlie, wait up," I blurted before I had a chance to stop myself. I wasn't exactly sure what I planned to say to her, but now the words were out of my mouth and I had to say *something*.

She stopped walking and turned towards me with a confused look on her face. "Yes?"

"Would you maybe want to hang out sometime outside of practice?" I paused for a brief moment to see what kind of reaction she would have. She didn't say anything, but her eyes widened in surprise. I took that as a good sign and continued. "I can show you around Jacksonville. Take you back to my place. Maybe make you a mean dinner, and then we can hang out and watch Netflix or something—"

She finally held up a hand to stop me. "Are you trying to hit on me?"

"Come on, I saw how you were looking at me this morning." I took a step closer to her. "Don't tell me you don't want this, too."

She put her hands on her hips and glared at me. "Do you talk to every girl like this?"

"Only the cute ones." I winked, taking another step towards her so that our bodies were only inches apart.

Our eyes met, and her glare slowly transformed into a smirk. "So, I'm supposed to be flattered, I take it?"

"Usually what happens." I took a lock of her wet hair and twirled it around one of my fingers. "Is it working on you?"

"Hmmm," she purred, and in a bold move, she pressed her breasts up against my chest. I took it as an invitation to check out her cleavage, and I liked what I was seeing.

I had her right where I wanted her.

I stole a glance around me, and Landon was the only one left on the pool deck. I didn't care if he saw me hitting on a teammate. I placed a hand on the small of Charlie's back and pulled the rest of her body tightly against mine. My body was reacting to her, and I pressed my hips into her so she could feel it. She raised her chin and leaned in as though she were going to kiss me but paused just before her lips touched mine.

"Should I take that as a yes?" I said in a husky voice. Lust was pumping through my veins and I wanted her. Bad.

The sweet scent of her hair mixed with chlorine filled my nostrils as she leaned in closer and brought her lips to my ear. "Not a chance, buddy," she whispered.

34

I felt the warmth of her body leave mine before I had a chance to register what she had said. She pursed her lips and turned around to head to the locker room once more.

"Hold on," I called to her, reality finally catching up to me. "What was *that*?"

She paused and turned to face me. "I guess the player isn't used to being played, huh?" She shook her head and laughed at me. "I'm sure plenty of other girls have fallen for your charm, Brody, but I promise you: I'm not one of them. Better luck next time." She winked and then disappeared into the women's locker room.

Landon appeared behind me and started laughing. "Are you trying to break a record of 'how many stupid things can Brody do in one week?' Because you're off to a pretty solid start!" I had told him what happened at Roman and Camila's Friday night over the weekend, so he knew about the mess I was in with that.

"Dude, shut up." I gave him a soft shove towards the locker room. "Like you could have done any better."

He snickered. "I would have been less of a pig."

"Whatever."

I wasn't used to being turned down, and I *really* wasn't used to feeling disappointed about being turned down. But despite the rejection, I still wanted Charlie. Instead of shrugging it off like usual, I felt something ignite inside me. It was an unfamiliar feeling I couldn't describe, but one thing was for sure: Charlie Price hadn't seen the last of me.

Chapter Four

Charlie

The morning swim workout had been tough, but it was nothing compared to our lifting session. We had 60 minutes of lifting, led by Coach Tanner, which worked every part of our body. Not only was I dripping in sweat, but I was pretty sure I wouldn't be able to move tomorrow. I had some intense workouts in college, but nothing like this—and I still had one more swim workout left today.

For a brief moment, I questioned what I had gotten myself into, but quickly threw that thought out of my mind. I knew this was going to take a lot of work, and my muscles would eventually adapt. I just needed to let my body adjust to the constant beating it would now be taking.

Instead of thinking about the pain, I distracted myself by thinking about the interaction I had with Brody this morning. What exactly had that been about? Did he do that to every new girl on the team? Maybe I should ask Allison if he did the same thing to her. She *was* going through the lifting circuit with me, and Brody was on the other side of the gym. It wouldn't be difficult to get a private word in with her.

But even if he *did* do this a lot, why did he assume I would be willing to jump on board so easily? Sure, he was attractive, and sure, I *accidentally* let my gaze linger a little too long on his rock-hard abs, but that did *not* mean I was willing to jump into bed with him the first day I met him. I wasn't sure if I should be offended that he thought I was easy, or laugh at the image of that smug look on his face when he thought he had won me over so quickly.

Either way, Brody Hayes better start getting used to somebody telling him no, because I had not worked this hard just to be humiliated by my own teammate.

"Were you counting?" Allison puffed, snapping me out of my thoughts. "I think that was twenty, right?"

"Erm, yes, I think so," I muttered. I forgot I was supposed to be spotting her on the bench press and counting how many reps she did.

She lowered the bar back down on the rack and let her arms dangle to the ground on either side of her. She looked up at me and chuckled. "It's okay if you lost track. I saw your face, you look distracted. Everything okay?"

"Oh, yeah, I'm fine. Just zoning out I guess," I lied. "How come Landon isn't lifting with us?" I asked to change the subject.

"I think Coach said he had a college tour today or something," she said as she sat up. "Typically, he does lift with us in the summer, but when school's in session he won't. His guidance counselor makes sure he's in some kind of PE class every semester that Coach counts as his lifting sessions. That way, he has time after school to work on homework before he comes back for his second swim in the evening.

"Brody usually swims the evening workout with him Monday, Wednesday, and Friday, and then I swim it with him on Tuesdays and Thursdays. Do you swim any of the evening practices?"

"No, all early afternoons," I told her. I stretched my arms, attempting to work out the kinks before my turn on the bench.

"It works out well then. Brody swims the afternoon practices on Tuesdays and Thursdays. Now, there will be two of us at each practice, and no one has to swim alone," she said as she got up and traded places with me. Once I was on the bench, she placed the bar in my hands.

Great. I get to swim alone with Brody twice a week. I only hoped he wouldn't try to hit on me again. I don't need things getting even more awkward than they already were.

It wasn't just the way he hit on me earlier that made me uncomfortable, but also the fact I wasn't ready to be in any kind of relationship right now—casual or serious. My college boyfriend and I broke up shortly before I left Minnesota. We had dated for almost three years, and I was certain he was the one. However, he didn't support my swimming dream, and I knew things needed to end. My heart still ached from that, and I knew it would be a while before I was ready to start over.

Instead of responding to Allison's comment, I focused on my task at hand. My arms wobbled slightly during the last few reps of the set, and I prayed we were almost done. My muscles desperately needed some rest if I had any hopes of making it through another swim workout today.

"Alright, that ought to do it for this morning. Good job guys." Coach Tanner turned off the music that had been blasting throughout the gym. I let out a sigh of relief that he had heard my silent prayer. "Allison and Charlie, I'll see you back at the pool at one. Brody, you'll be back at six to swim with Landon?"

Brody came walking up from somewhere behind us. He was shirtless and wiping sweat off his forehead with a towel. "Yes sir, I'll be here."

I shook my head ferociously when I once again caught myself staring too long. Thankfully, he didn't seem to notice this time, but I really needed to start watching myself around him. I didn't want my lingering eye to get me further into trouble.

"Good. Ladies, make sure you eat a filling lunch." Coach looked at Allison and me. "You're going to need fuel for your second swim." He gathered up his things and waved to us as he left the gym.

Allison sat down on a bench beside me and took a long swig from her water bottle. Maybe now was a good time to ask her about Brody. I should find out if she had any thoughts on his behavior. Brody was still far enough away that he probably wouldn't hear.

Taking a step closer to her, I decided to go for it. "Hey, Allison, I've got a question for you."

She looked up at me expectantly. "Sure, what's up?"

"I was wondering—"

"Allison, you hit 240 on the squat rack, yet?" Brody suddenly appeared at our side, interrupting me.

Well, so much for that.

"I got up to 230 this morning." She pretended to pout. "I'm so close, yet so far!"

"230 is still solid. You'll make your goal in no time. I have no doubt about it." He gave her a high five which she happily accepted.

"Thanks, bro. Charlie here might beat 240 pretty soon, too at the rate she's going." She pointed to me, and I felt Brody's eyes on me before I even looked at him. "She squatted 220 this morning."

His eyebrows raised ever so slightly and if I wasn't mistaken, I'd almost say he was impressed.

"I had a feeling she would be a force to be reckoned with," he said. "I even told Coach Tanner I was super impressed with her already."

I narrowed my eyes at him, not sure if he was serious or not. He didn't actually say anything to Coach about me. Did he?

"I was watching you swim this morning, Charlie," he continued. "I get the feeling you're not one to turn down a good challenge. Swimming or otherwise." He winked at me.

"Depends on the challenge," I said without missing a beat. "If I'm going to get nothing out of it, then I don't usually waste my time."

He looked away from me then, but I could tell he was trying to hide a smile.

Allison sat between us looking from me, to Brody, and back to me again. "Am I missing something here?"

"No," Brody chuckled. "I'll see you ladies tomorrow." His gaze lingered on me for a beat longer before he finally walked past us to the locker room.

"That was weird," Allison muttered. "Anyway, Charlie, you wanted to ask me something?"

"Oh, right." The interruption from Brody had distracted me, and now I wasn't sure I wanted to talk about what had happened anymore. Allison did call Brody "bro," so maybe they had a more brother/sister relationship. But "bro" was also the first part of Brody's name—

"Charlie?" Allison asked again, looking slightly concerned.

"Sorry! My brain is everywhere today." I shook my head, embarrassed at myself for acting so strange. "I, uh, was wondering if you wanted to grab lunch today?" That was a good cover-up.

She laughed. "I understand, today's been a big change for you." She stood up and wrapped her sweat towel around her neck. "I actually picked up an extra shift over lunch today. I'm a personal trainer at another gym in town. Wednesday I'm free though, if you want to grab something then?"

"Yeah, that would be great." I smiled. I needed to start making some friends out here anyway, so this actually worked out pretty well.

"Perfect, give me your number so we can make plans. Maybe you can tell me what's going on between you and Brody, too."

I shrugged. "Maybe."

However, I realized if Brody's behavior came off as strange to Allison, then I think my earlier question had been answered: Brody obviously didn't act that way around just *anyone.*

******

I let out a sigh of relief when I finished the last swim of my first day. The second swim was a little better than the morning workout, if only because Brody wasn't there to make things awkward. However, the workout itself was just as brutal as the morning session, and I was in dire need of a nap.

When I pulled myself out of the pool, I wrapped a towel around my waist, and sat down in the stands to rest for a moment. Allison was already out of the water as well, rapidly gathering her things beside me.

"Hey, I have to run back to work, but I wanted to say you did really well today, Charlie," she said with a wide smile. "You're going to be a very valuable member of our team, and I'm so glad you're here."

"Thank you." I blushed. "That means the world to me. I'm thrilled to be here."

"Get some rest before tomorrow, I'll see you later!" She waved to me as she hurried into the locker room to change.

"I agree with Allison," Coach Tanner said. He took a seat beside me on the bench. "You have gotten much stronger since the last time I saw you, Charlie. I'm very impressed."

"I've been working my ass off. I didn't want you to regret your decision in choosing me."

Coach tipped his head back and laughed. "Well, I haven't regretted it yet. I think you are going to be a force to be reckoned with once you start competing. The meet in Miami this weekend should be exciting. I'm glad I was able to squeeze you in."

"Thanks, Coach, I'm excited to see how it goes." I smiled to myself. It felt really good to have my new coach and my teammates have so much faith in me.

"So, I remember over one of our phone calls that you said you were planning to get another job once you were out here," Coach said. "Have you found anything yet?"

"Not yet. I was going to start my search this afternoon."

"If you need any help, let me know. I might be able to give you a few names. Just don't kill yourself trying to find something this week. This first week especially is going to wear you out, and you need to get plenty of rest. Especially with a meet only a few days away."

"You got it, Coach. Nap first, job search second," I joked.

"Atta girl." He grinned. "How's everything going otherwise? Getting along with everyone?"

"Allison and Landon are great," I said, purposely leaving Brody out of the equation.

It didn't get past him, though. His eyes narrowed before he spoke. "What about Brody?"

My mind immediately went back to the interaction Brody and I had this morning. As much as I wanted to put it out of my mind, I couldn't stop thinking about it all day. Coach Tanner clearly knew him better than I did. Maybe he could shed some light on the subject.

"We certainly had an interesting first introduction." I fiddled with the edge of my towel so I could avoid looking at him. "I'm not sure we'll be best friends anytime soon."

He sighed and shook his head. "I'm sorry. I don't know what to do with him sometimes. He's a great guy—he really is—he just doesn't always make the best first impressions. It took a while for Allison and Landon to come around to him, too, but now they all get along great. Brody's pretty picky about who he gets close to."

"Why?"

"He's always been that way." He shrugged. "At least for as long as I've known him. I'm sure not having his parents around has contributed to that."

"Where are his parents?" My head snapped up to look Coach Tanner in the eye.

He sighed. "He doesn't like to talk about it, but they passed away a few years ago in a car accident."

"That's awful," I whispered. My parents were my rocks, I couldn't imagine what it would be like to lose both of them, and at such a young age, too.

"It is, but that kind of thing can change a person. Anyway, the point I'm trying to make is that you should just be patient with him.

41

He'll come around once he gets to know you. There's no way he isn't going to like you."

"And if he doesn't come around?"

"We'll cross that bridge if we get there." He winked. "Well, I better go get some work done before those boys get back here tonight. I'll see you bright and early in the morning." He gave my shoulder a pat before he took off in the direction of his office.

I sat a minute longer by myself to collect my thoughts. Coach Tanner obviously knew Brody better than I did, but what if he was wrong? What if Brody already decided he wanted nothing to do with me? Maybe he thought hitting on me was a surefire way to make sure I left him alone, and if that was the case, what else would he do to drive me away? Would I eventually have to switch teams?

No.

That was one thing I wouldn't do. I had just as much of a right to be on this team as he did. I worked my butt off for this, and I wasn't going to let someone like him ruin it. I made a vow to myself a long time ago that I would do whatever it took to become a professional swimmer, and nothing was going to prevent me from being the best swimmer I could be.

Not even Brody Hayes.

******

When I got home after practice, I decided a phone call to my parents was in order. I still couldn't get Brody off my mind, and thinking about the death of his parents made me want to reach out and check in on mine. They'd probably still be out working, but since harvest season didn't start for a little while yet, I was hopeful I could steal them away for a few minutes.

"Charlie, dear?" My mom said when she answered the phone. "How is your first day going? Tell me all about it."

"It's great, Mom, but I'm definitely going to be sore tomorrow," I chuckled. "Is Dad around, too?"

"Yes, he is. I'll put you on speaker." There was a brief silence while she figured out how to adjust the phone. "Can you hear us?"

"Yes, I can hear you." I smiled into the phone. "Hey Dad!"

"Hey kiddo!" His deep voice came from the other end. "So, the first day is going well, huh?"

42

"Yeah, the workouts were intense, but I knew that would be the case. My teammates seem nice. Allison and I are going to get lunch together on Wednesday."

"That's great!" My mom squealed. "I'm so excited for you. She's the only other girl, right?"

"Yes, she is."

"What about the boys?" My dad asked. "Are they nice, too?"

"One of them is pretty quiet, and I only had one workout with him, so didn't really get to talk to him. Brody Hayes is the other guy on my team."

"Oh, please tell me about him," my mom said. "Is he as great as we always thought? He looks awfully handsome in that poster you had in your dorm room."

I grimaced at the thought of Brody finding out I had a poster of him. "I'm pretty sure I left that in my room at home. You can throw it away."

"What? Why would we do that?" my dad asked. "Did something happen today?"

"He just tried to hit on me," I said. Not wanting my overprotective father to hop on the next flight to Florida, I didn't think it was necessary to be more specific than that.

"Honey, why is that a bad thing?" my mom asked, a hint of concern in her voice.

"Seriously, Mom? Nick and I literally just broke up. I'm still trying to get over that." I was also certain she wouldn't be saying that if she knew *how* he'd hit on me.

"Nick has no idea how good he had it," my mom said. "You deserve someone who will chase after your dreams with you, instead of holding you back."

My throat tightened and I felt tears forming in the back of my eyes. The breakup was still raw and thinking about it wasn't easy. The day Nick tried to convince me to back out of coming to Jacksonville and get a "real job" was one of the worst days of my life. The whole time we had been together, I thought he supported my dream, but it turned out, he was secretly hoping it wouldn't work out or I would change my mind. It made me question the entire relationship, and I wondered if I had really known Nick at all.

"Honey, are you still there?" my dad asked after a moment.

43

Sniffing back the tears, I instinctively nodded. "Yes, I'm here," I said when I remembered they couldn't see me. "I just don't think I'm going to be ready for another relationship for a while. My heart still hurts from the last one."

"I know, honey," my mom said. "But don't turn someone away who may be genuinely interested. You never know what could happen."

"Just take it one day at a time, kiddo. Wish I could give you a hug right now."

"Me too, Dad."

We talked a little longer about what was going on back home, but I wasn't fully present for the conversation. I kept thinking about what my mom had said about Brody genuinely liking me. I wanted to tell her she was wrong, that Brody didn't like me at all. At least, that's what I had interpreted from talking to Coach Tanner.

Did I misunderstand? Could it be possible that Brody just didn't know how to talk to a new girl without sounding like a jerk? I honestly didn't know what to think anymore.

It really didn't matter though. Whether Brody was genuinely interested or not, I wasn't going to pursue anything with him. I had a career to worry about, and I wasn't going to let a boy get in my head and ruin it.

Chapter Five

Brody

"Hey guys, I need to go," I said after I glanced at the clock and noticed it was already almost 2:30. If I didn't leave now, I'd be late getting over to Roman's house. "Do you have enough photos to work with?"

"Yeah, we should be good Brody, we'll have you come back tomorrow if we need more. Same time?" asked Mike, my manager. We were in the middle of a photoshoot for a magazine article on the new tech suits that Speedo was coming out with. I had been posing on a starting block that was positioned in front of a green screen with the new suit. Luckily, as part of my pay for the article, I got to keep it, and I couldn't wait to see how well it performed in the water.

"No, I have an afternoon practice tomorrow," I told him. "What about Wednesday?"

"Works for us. Thanks for today, and I'll be in touch about future projects." He gave me a fist bump on my way out.

I needed to step on it. I didn't need to piss Roman off more than I already had.

Hustling to the changing room, I grabbed a bottle of water and a cookie off the snack table as I went by. In record time, I had changed, gathered all my belongings, and was on my way out of the building. Once in my truck, I glanced at the clock: 2:46. I was going to be late regardless now, so I didn't bother to drive recklessly.

It was shortly after three when I stopped my truck in the same spot the Audi had been parked last Friday. I grumbled to myself as I made my way up the ridiculously long driveway and rang the doorbell.

A moment later, Camila answered the door, her phone pressed up against one ear, but holding her fingers wide as if she had just finished painting her nails. "Oh, it's you," she said coolly when she saw me.

"Were you expecting someone else?" I turned to look behind me as if someone else would be walking up the driveway towards us. "Roman said he wanted me here at three today."

"Right," she said to me, then into the phone, "I'll have to call you back later … yes, I'm working on it … I can't talk about it right now … bye." She hung up the phone and motioned for me to follow her inside.

"Was that Roman you were talking to?" I asked, closing the door behind me once I was inside.

"No, he's in a meeting." She kept walking down the hallway and didn't offer any further explanation.

Instead of pushing for more, I followed her in silence. We passed by the life-sized portrait of her at the end of the hall, and I once again had to resist rolling my eyes. We continued walking through what I assumed was the dining room. A long wooden table with enough chairs to fit at least a dozen people took up most of the room.

Beyond that was another sitting room, this one held brown leather furniture that actually looked comfortable—compared to the old, dainty blue furniture I had to sit on the last time I was here—and a huge flat-screen TV took up most of the wall. It was a room I would probably enjoy spending time in if I actually wanted to be here.

Finally, she led me to the opposite end of the house to a room with an entire wall made of glass. I could see out into the backyard, where they had a pool and a hot tub set up, as well as several lawn chairs. It looked as though they had their own private spa out back. Camila went to the sliding door on one end of the glass wall and led me outside.

"You will start by emptying the pool, and then you will scrub it clean. Once that's done, you can give it a new coat of paint as well." Camila strolled out to the grass and pointed a freshly manicured hand to the pool, and then motioned over to the hot tub. "Then do the same with the hot tub when you're finished. Everything you need has been set out for you."

"So, is the pool already being drained?" I had a feeling I already knew the answer since there was still plenty of water in it, but asked anyway.

She gave me a disgusted look. "No, that's what you're here for."

"Okay, but it's going to take a while to drain. Is there anything you want me to do in the meantime, or should I sit here and fiddle my thumbs?"

Her eyes widened as she realized the situation. "I didn't think of that …"

"Clearly," I mumbled, just loud enough for her to hear.

She glared at me and crossed her arms. "Look, I want you here as much as you want to be here, Brody. I wish Roman would have just taken the buyout. I don't need you snooping around my home."

"Do you think I'd find anything interesting?" I was joking, but the look on her face told me she didn't find it very funny. I held my hands up in surrender. "Loosen up, will ya? I was only messing around—"

"Just get to work. I have my own work to get to." She turned and started back towards the glass door. "You can wipe down all the lawn chairs while you wait for the pool to drain." She closed the door behind her and disappeared into the house.

I groaned and got to work. I was almost finished wiping down the lawn chairs, and the pool was only half empty when one of Roman's maids opened the glass door and came out dragging behind her a massive laundry basket.

"Brody, right?" the woman asked when she approached me. She had to have been close to the same age as Penelope—the maid from Friday night—and her short, brown hair was trimmed into a bob around her chin.

Looking up from the lawn chair I was wiping down, I shot her a smile. "Yeah, that's me."

"Great. Camila told us to find something for you to do while the pool drained." She slid the laundry basket in front of me. "I've got other things to do, so would you mind folding her laundry for me?"

My smile disappeared and I was instantly annoyed. "Yeah, just leave it there." I went back to scrubbing and the maid vanished back into the house a moment later.

Once the chairs were clean, I pulled the basket up to one of them and took a seat to start folding. This was humiliating. Next, she'd start making me wear a uniform or something.

To distract myself, I started thinking about Charlie. She was a feisty one, but I kind of liked it. That probably meant she was crazy in bed, too. I imagined what it would be like: my hands running over her luscious curves and kissing her until her lips were swollen. Remembering the warmth of her body when it was pressed up against mine earlier today only added fuel to the lust I felt for her.

47

God, I wanted her.

I was brought out of my daydream when something small and hard fell out of the pair of pants I was folding. Picking it up off the cement, I noticed it was a flash drive. Camila would probably want this back. Sticking it in my pocket, I put the folded laundry back into the basket, and decided the pool was empty enough to start cleaning.

The water level was a little more than ankle-deep yet, so I removed my socks and shoes and went into the water to start scrubbing the walls of the pool.

I worked for over an hour, and managed to get the pool completely drained, and somewhat clean. I definitely wouldn't have a chance to start painting, as it was almost time to get back for my second swim.

After cleaning up the supplies and putting them back where I found them, I decided I'd go inside and hit the bathroom before taking off. However, Camila never showed me where one was, and there weren't any maids in sight, so I had to guess. I opened a few doors, but they were all bedrooms. I went to try another door, but as soon as I turned the knob, the door swung open, and Camila was staring back at me from the other side.

"What are you doing?" The color drained from her face.

"I was looking for the bathroom. You didn't show me where it was."

"Well, this isn't it." She took a step forward, shoved me out of the way, and closed the door tightly behind her. "This room is strictly off-limits."

"Why? Are you hiding something?" I scoffed. I was joking again, simply trying to push her buttons, but it set her off.

"I'm not hiding anything," she barked. "This is my bedroom. I don't want you in *my* bedroom."

"You mean yours and Roman's, right?"

"Yes, of course that's what I meant." She was flustered. She wouldn't look at me, and she couldn't hold still.

Something was up. Did she forget we used to date? I had been in her bedroom at her old place. I'd seen all her stuff before, including all her "private" stuff. It's not like it was any kind of secret to me. Why was she suddenly panicking about me going in her room? *Was* she hiding something?

I narrowed my eyes. "Is something going on?"

"It's really none of your business anymore, Brody," she snapped. "Roman should be home any minute now. When he gets here, I'm going to demand that he dismiss you. I don't want you in my home anymore."

"Whatever." I shrugged. "By the way, I found this while folding laundry." I took the flash drive out of my pocket and handed it to her. When she saw it, her mouth dropped open before she quickly snatched it out of my grasp.

"Thank God," she whispered, clutching the thing to her chest. "I've been looking everywhere for this."

"Should probably keep better track of your shit."

Her glare returned in an instant, but before she could respond, the front door opened, and we heard Roman shout a greeting as he walked in.

She shot me a warning glance before she stepped around me. "Roman, we need to talk."

I followed her to the front door in silence. She didn't invite me to follow, but I wanted to be there to defend myself against whatever she was going to tell him.

He sighed when he saw Camila marching towards him. "What is it my dear?" He tried to lean in and give her a kiss, but she held him at arm's length.

"I don't want Brody in my house anymore!"

"*Our* house," he said calmly.

She ignored him and continued to yell. "I caught him snooping around—"

"I was looking for a bathroom."

"It doesn't matter!" Camila shrieked. "He was about to go into a private room, and I don't want that to happen anymore."

"You said earlier it was your bedroom," I reminded her. "Roman, I wasn't trying to pry. Really, I was just looking for a bathroom."

"Wait, our bedroom?" Roman looked at Camila with a puzzled look, and then turned his attention back to me. "Brody, what were you doing on the third floor? I thought you would be out back cleaning the pool today."

"I was out back. I never went on any other floor besides this one."

"Well, our bedroom is on the third floor." Roman looked to Camila once more for an explanation.

There was definitely something going on with Camila. She had to be hiding something. I was almost certain of it now. But what?

"Please, Roman," Camila brought her voice down several octaves, as she pleaded with him. "Take the buyout. I don't want him here."

"I'm sorry, Camila, but I want to teach him a lesson." He folded his arms over his chest. "I'm afraid you're just going to have to accept that he will be here for a while."

"UGH!" She screamed, stomping her foot and clenching her fists. She looked like a five-year-old girl having a meltdown. "This isn't over!" She stomped away, this time up the stairs, towards what I assumed was her actual bedroom.

"Terribly sorry about that," Roman said. "Although, you know how she is. I shouldn't have to apologize to you."

I raised my eyebrows in agreement. "I should probably be going. When do you want me back?"

"Tomorrow. Same time would be great. Let me show you where the bathroom is before you go, so we can avoid another episode like this."

Once Roman had shown me where all the bathrooms were—the ones I was allowed to use anyway—I excused myself and took off for the pool.

During the drive, I thought about what had happened. Camila had been acting stranger than usual, and I wondered what she was up to. After a minute, I decided not to dwell on it. After all, it was Camila we were talking about here. She wasn't dumb, but she was certainly no genius. Whatever she was up to, it couldn't be *that* bad, right?

******

When I arrived at the pool, Landon was sitting on one of the benches with his head down. Wanting to tell him about what happened, I immediately made my way over.

"You'll never believe what happened at Roman's house today," I said when I reached him.

50

"What?" His voice was completely void of any emotion, and he didn't look up when he spoke. In fact, he turned his head away from me as if something across the room had caught his attention.

"You okay?" I asked, craning my neck in an attempt to look at his face.

"Yeah, I'm fine." He still didn't look up. "What happened at Roman's?"

Reaching for his shoulder, I tried to turn him towards me. "Hey, look at me. What's going on?"

I stopped in my tracks. He finally looked me in the eye, and I was shocked speechless. His left eye was black and blue, and nearly swollen shut.

"Don't worry about it." Landon tried to cover his eye with his hand and turned away from me once more.

"What the hell happened?" I pulled his arm away from his face in order to get a better look.

"Brody, it's not a big deal. Just drop it."

"Who did this to you? I'm going to beat the shit out of them." My face burned red with anger.

"Let it go—"

"Who did this to you?" I said a little more sternly.

Surrendering, Landon let out a long sigh. "I went on a tour of Jacksonville University today. I had to stop by my house before I came here to drop off my things, and my dad was home early."

"Are you saying your dad did this to you?"

Landon said nothing. He looked away, but not before I saw a tear run down his cheek.

Damn. I knew Landon's father was terrible, I even had suspicions that he had hit Landon before, but seeing it in the flesh was different.

I ran a hand through my hair and cursed under my breath. "Tell me what happened, Landon."

"I took the bus home after the tour. My dad didn't want to come with me and I didn't have a ride." His voice cracked as he spoke, and it was clear he was trying to hold back more tears. "I asked my dad for a ride when I got home. He said he had a bad day at work and didn't have time to take me to practice, so I asked for a little more money to take the bus again. He became furious, saying I

51

was always asking for money, and I never appreciate it. He was yelling a lot, and throwing things around, and he … hit me.

"I got scared, so I ran out of there." He cleared his throat before continuing. "I was going to call you, but I didn't know if you were done at Roman's or not, so I was just going to start walking. Eventually, someone from school saw me walking and offered to give me a ride. Luckily, he didn't ask any questions about my face."

I clenched my fists at my side, and anger swirled in my gut. "You're staying at my place for a few days. I'm not taking no for an answer."

He nodded, but didn't say anything more.

I couldn't wait until Landon turned eighteen and he could leave his dad in the dust. I've asked him a bunch of times why he never told the cops about the way his father treated him. He always told me that he wouldn't be able to live with himself if he did. Maybe he hoped his dad would eventually treat him like a decent human being—like a son. However, Landon told me this had been going on ever since his mom died, and Landon was only six when that happened. If Mr. Davis wasn't treating his own son with some decency after eleven years, I wasn't convinced it was ever going to happen.

"Do you think you can still put your goggles on and make it through practice?" I asked him.

His shoulders sagged. "I don't know. I'm not really looking forward to explaining this to Coach Tanner."

As if on cue, Coach Tanner came strolling out of his office a moment later. He was typing on his phone as he walked, so he didn't see Landon's face until he was standing right in front of us.

His expression darkened immediately. "What the hell? What happened?"

Landon looked to me as if he didn't know what to say.

"It was my fault," I blurted, turning towards Coach Tanner. "Well, an accident, really. It was so nice out this afternoon, Landon and I were throwing the ball around after his college tour. He tried to catch the ball with his face."

Landon let out a sigh of relief. "Yep, that's what happened."

Coach Tanner shook his head, and then leaned in closer to examine Landon's face. "You two need to be more careful. Come on, let's get some ice on that."

52

I watched as they walked away in silence. Wringing my hands together, I tried to keep my cool instead of screaming or hitting something. Landon was like a little brother to me, and I hated that he was in this situation. I hated Mr. Davis, and I hated that Landon wouldn't do anything about the way his dad treated him.

Frustrated, I decided to jump in the water and start my warm up before I ditched practice to give Landon's dad a taste of his own medicine.

Chapter Six

Charlie

I woke up the next morning feeling as though I had been hit by a bus. Everything was sore. I knew there was a chance I would be a bit stiff after my first day of intense training, but I was surprised at just how sore I actually was. It's not like I hadn't had tough practices in the past, but to be fair, working out wasn't my full-time job before now.

Even so, I welcomed the aches and pains, as they provided a much-needed distraction from thinking about Brody—if only for a little while. While I tried my best not to think about him, I couldn't stop replaying our introduction in my head. I was still going back and forth about what his intentions were yesterday.

Obviously, he had been a bit too forward with me, and at the time, I wasn't thrilled about it at all. However, the more I thought about it, the more I thought maybe I should take it as a compliment.

He was Brody Hayes, after all, and girls all over the country gushed over his devilishly good looks and charm. And even though I wasn't the type of girl to jump into bed with someone I just met, it was almost kind of flattering that he wanted me.

Did that sound crazy? Probably.

Either way, it didn't really matter. I wasn't interested, and nothing was going to happen. *Stop thinking about him.*

I got to the pool early this morning for the first workout, and groaned when I saw Brody was already there stretching on deck. I was hoping I'd have some time to mentally prepare myself for whatever he was going to do today. Was he going to try and hit on me again?

Whatever. Bring your worst, Brody. I was ready.

He smiled and said hello when he saw me, and I gave him a wave before I set my things down on the bleachers and started pulling my equipment out of my bag.

"Charlie, how are you this morning?" he asked.

I turned to face him. "I'm fine. How are you?"

His hands were laced together behind his back as he took a few slow steps in my direction. "Doing well. Listen, there's something I wanted to tell you."

"What's that?" I asked. *Where was he going with this?*

"I was thinking about your freestyle technique last night, and I think there are a few things you could improve on."

"Is that so?" I turned away from him to hide my eye roll and went back to unpacking my things. Coach Tanner would have said something if there was anything wrong with my technique.

"Yeah, I think if you were to bend your elbows just a touch more than you're currently doing, and make less of an 'S' shape with your pull, you'd improve your times and be much quicker." He was now standing right next to me, and he reached out and grabbed both of my arms. "Here, I can show you."

I jerked both of my arms out of his grip and took a step back. "Brody, I don't need you to show me anything, I'm doing just fine."

"Don't you want to swim faster?"

"Didn't you say just yesterday that you were impressed with my swimming? Why didn't you say something about my stroke then?" I crossed my arms and raised my eyebrows.

"Well, I've had more time to think about it since then," he argued. "I just want everyone on this team to be the best swimmer they can be. If you want to keep swimming with sloppy technique, then be my guest."

"My sloppy technique has gotten me this far, hasn't it?"

"And imagine how much farther you could get if you'd let me help you." He was so close I could feel the heat of his breath on my face.

My blood was boiling and I opened my mouth to shout at him some more, when I realized that's what he wanted me to do. He was testing me again, and I was letting him. I snapped my mouth shut and turned my head to gather my bearings.

When I looked back at him, I tried to give him a sweet smile. "Thanks, Brody. I'll keep your suggestions in mind." I turned and walked away from him before he could say anything else. I was going to have the last word in this conversation. Stopping a couple yards away, I started stretching on my own to prepare for practice.

Luckily, Allison came out of the locker room a moment later, and I smiled when she looked my way.

"Good morning, Allison," I said as she approached.

"Hey! How are you feeling today?"

"Sore," I chuckled. "I think an ice bath may be in my future."

"Get a massage, too, if you have time. That will help tremendously." She set her stuff down next to mine. "Listen, I've been thinking about what Brody said to you yesterday after the lifting session."

Here we go.

"I wouldn't put too much thought into it," I said quickly. "I don't think he meant anything by it."

"I wouldn't be so sure." She smirked. "There was definitely some sexual tension there. I could feel it."

I laughed even though I wanted to roll my eyes again. "Whatever you say."

"I'm just calling it as I see it." She shrugged. "But I've been wrong before. However, I will have you know, that I strongly believe whoever ends up with Brody will be one lucky girl. Something to keep in mind."

"Right," I scoffed. "I don't think it'll be me, Allison. In fact, if I knew who it was, I'd warn her. Let her know what she's getting herself into."

"Oh, you're too hard on him," she scolded. "Give him a chance, you've only just met him. He can be a bit thick-headed, but he can be a sweetheart, too. You'll see."

I smiled, but didn't respond. I continued my stretches as I pondered her words. Not thinking about Brody was proving to be much easier said than done. How was I supposed to get him off my mind, if every conversation I had with someone was going to involve him in some way?

Coach Tanner saved me from my own thoughts for a brief moment when he popped out of his office and told us to get in and start warming up. That brief moment didn't last past the warm up though, because Coach put Brody in my lane for the main set, making it especially difficult to *not* think about him.

The entire practice, I tried to ignore the fact that I could feel him watching me. He was probably picking apart my every move, trying to find something else wrong with my technique. It made me pay extra close attention to how I swam, because I wasn't going to give him the satisfaction of finding something to nitpick. I was a damn good swimmer, even if I was new to this team. I wasn't going to let Brody make me think otherwise.

During the lifting session, I was able to pair up with Allison and we went and did our own thing without Brody. Landon was with us today, so the two of them were on the other side of the gym. Allison tried to go on about how great Brody was again, but I quickly put a stop to that. I just wanted a few minutes that didn't involve thinking or talking about him.

Suddenly, the music in the gym stopped playing. "Would all of you please come here for a moment?" Coach Tanner called us over. "I'm afraid I have some bad news."

"What's going on?" Allison asked once we were all together.

"I was just on the phone with Roman, and unfortunately, when he went to submit the funds for our swim meet this weekend, he discovered one of his bank accounts had been depleted."

"What?" Allison and I said in unison.

"Apparently, someone was able to hack into his security system, and wiped him out," Coach continued. "He's shutting down operations for the time being, until he can find out what happened. So unfortunately, that means our funding for the meet in Miami this weekend has fallen through."

"Can't we get another sponsor to cover it?" Landon asked, disappointment written all over his face.

"I'm afraid it's a bit late to ask another sponsor for extra funds," Coach said. "They all have pretty strict budget plans. We can't throw them for a loop in the middle of the fiscal year."

"Roman's got more than enough personal money to pay the dues," Brody grumbled. "He could easily donate a little if he wanted to prove he was a good sponsor—"

"He *is* a good sponsor, Brody." Coach interrupted. "How would you feel if I asked you to fork over your personal funds after your company had been robbed? I know you don't like the man, but you can be respectful."

"How did his company get broken into?" Allison asked. "They're a cybersecurity company. Shouldn't they have the best kind of security in place for situations just like this?"

"He doesn't know. Could be an inside job for all we know." He shrugged. "I'm so sorry about the meet, guys. I know you've been working hard. I talked to the sponsor who is covering the funds for our Atlanta meet, and they assured me we were covered. We'll make up for it there. It'll just be a few weeks later than planned."

My heart sank a little knowing I would have to wait even longer before I could compete. I was so excited to go down to Miami and show everyone what I was capable of. I understood why Roman couldn't give us the funds anymore, but it was still disappointing.

"Go ahead and call it a day on the strength exercises," Coach Tanner said. "Get some rest before your last swim for the day." He packed up his things and left the room a moment later.

"What do you think happened?" Allison asked. "Seems kind of suspicious, doesn't it?"

"A bit, yeah." Brody wiped his face with a towel and went about gathering his things. "Maybe I can ask him about it this evening."

"Why are you seeing Roman tonight?" I asked him.

He froze for a moment, as if he had said something he wasn't supposed to. "Uh, I'm not. Sorry," he said quickly. "I thought you were talking about someone else. Let's go, Landon." He sped off to the locker room with Landon following shortly behind him before Allison or I could ask any other questions.

"That was also a little suspicious," Allison said quietly. "Maybe you could talk to him during your swim this afternoon?"

"I doubt he'd tell me anything."

"Worth a try, I suppose." She shrugged. "Something weird is going on."

I had yet to meet this Roman guy, but I had to admit something felt a bit off with Brody. After our little spat this morning, I wasn't thrilled about having to talk to him one-on-one again, but I agreed to ask him about it and get to the bottom of whatever was going on.

******

Fifteen minutes before the afternoon practice was supposed to start, I was on the pool deck stretching and going over in my head what I was going to say to Brody. When he finally came out of the locker room, our eyes met, and my initial instinct was to quickly look away. I shook my head and mentally told myself to suck it up and just get it over with. Even though I told myself I was asking for Allison, I was curious too. While making my way over to him, I repeatedly reminded myself to stay calm and not let him get to me.

"Hey Charlie," he said smoothly when I had reached him.

"Hey. Look, I need to ask you something," I said.

"Does it have anything to do with Roman's data breach?" he sighed. "Because I don't know anything more than you do."

"But why did you say you were going to talk to Roman tonight? How often do you see him?"

"What do you think the main set will be this afternoon?" he asked, more to himself than to me.

"Brody, don't change the subject." I was getting annoyed.

"How have you been enjoying the practices so far?"

"Brody!" I crossed my arms and glared at him. Was he even hearing me?

"I imagine you were probably pretty sore when you woke up this morning." He smirked. He knew exactly what he was doing.

"Yes, I was." I rolled my eyes. "Can you answer the question I asked?"

"You could use ice or heat to help, but you probably already know that."

I gave up. He wasn't going to answer me.

"I do know that. I iced last night." I finally decided to walk away from him and went for my swim bag lying on the bleachers.

"Well, that would explain why you've been acting so cold," he called after me.

My mouth dropped open. Was he serious right now? *He* was going to give *me* attitude? I turned to tell him off but shut my mouth when I saw the smallest hint of a smile on his lips.

"Are you trying to make fun of me?" I asked, growing even more annoyed.

His lips turned up into a full smile. "I wouldn't dare make fun of you."

"You need to stop."

The smile disappeared and he feigned confusion. "Stop what?"

"This." I waved my arms in front of me for emphasis. "You need to stop messing with my head. Yesterday, you were hitting on me. Earlier today, you told me I suck at swimming, and now you're making fun of me. What are you trying to accomplish here, Brody? Why are you trying to push me away?"

"I'm not trying—"

"It doesn't matter, because guess what, buddy? I don't care if you like me or not. You're just going to have to put up with me. I worked hard to get here, and I'm not going to let someone like you ruin this for me." I turned and walked away before he could say anything else. Screw getting answers for Allison. She could ask him herself.

Once I reached my bag on the bleachers, I started pulling out my equipment, and angrily muttering nonsense under my breath. After a moment, I felt someone appear at my side.

"I'm sorry," Brody said softly.

I stopped what I was doing and turned my gaze to him.

"I'm not trying to push you away," he said, looking me in the eye.

Narrowing my eyes, I didn't respond. Instead, I waited for him to explain.

"Yesterday, I may have gone a touch too far," he continued. "I could have sworn I saw you checking me out, and I thought we had the same thing in mind."

"Even if I *was* checking you out, that doesn't mean—"

"I know," he interrupted. "And I'm sorry. I'm not going to lie, Charlie, I'm attracted to you. I thought I'd get over it when you turned me down, but I literally haven't been able to stop thinking about you since you first walked in the door. That's not a feeling I'm used to having. I wanted to talk to you more, but I'll also admit I'm not very good at making conversation. Sometimes, I come off the wrong way and I don't mean to."

I raised an eyebrow. "So, you don't think I suck at swimming?"

"Obviously, you don't, or you wouldn't be here," he chuckled. "I do think you could tweak a few things, though."

Frowning, I opened my mouth to argue, but he held his hand up to stop me.

"I'm not saying that to be mean. Coach Tanner wanted to fix my stroke when I came on board, too. But, if you'd prefer I don't help you, then I won't." He shrugged. "I do want to get to know you better, though, and maybe redeem myself from the last few days."

"Well, I'm not sure if I would get my hopes up if I were you," I said.

He frowned. "Why not?"

60

"Because you dug yourself quite the hole yesterday." I turned my attention back to my swim bag, pulling out the last pieces of my equipment. "It's going to take a lot of work to get yourself out."

He chuckled, which forced me to look back at him to see what was so funny.

"One thing you'll soon find out about me, Charlie, is that when I want something, I don't stop working at it until it's mine. Hard work doesn't scare me." He winked and walked away before I could say anything more.

Tempted to say something further, I turned around to call after him, but clamped my mouth shut when I saw Coach Tanner coming out of his office towards us. Now wasn't the time to argue, but this conversation was far from over.

"How's it going?" Coach Tanner asked as he walked up to us. He probably just wanted to make sure Brody wasn't being an ass again after what I told him yesterday.

"Everything's great," I said. It wasn't a total lie, but not really the truth either.

Coach Tanner looked from me to Brody, and back again. "Alright, so are we ready to get started?"

I nodded. "Ready whenever you are, Coach." I tried to steal another glance at Brody, but he was pulling his goggles over his head, paying no attention to me.

"Go ahead and start with a fifteen-minute warm up on your own," Coach Tanner said. "I've got a fun practice for you this afternoon, so make sure you are good and loosened up."

Throughout the workout, I replayed my conversation with Brody over again in my mind. He said he didn't stop working until he had what he wanted. Did that mean he wasn't going to stop until he had me? And in what way did he mean? Did he just want to sleep with me, or did he actually want something more? Honestly, the more I thought about it, the more questions I had.

Clearly, I didn't know Brody that well yet—and I could be way off—but something about the way he looked at me told me he wanted something with me. Something more than a friendship or casual hookup, and that made me nervous.

"Charlie, did you hear me?" Coach Tanner's voice pulled me from my thoughts.

I shook my head. We were in between sets, and Brody and I were resting on the wall. "I'm sorry, what did you say?"

"Come on, girl, get your head in it. I asked if you thought you could make ten 100's on the 1:05, all freestyle."

I grimaced, but nodded. "I will try."

"Bump it up to 1:10 if you need to, but I want high intensity, low rest. Both of you start at the top of the clock."

I forced myself to focus all my energy on the rest of the workout, and was able to make all ten 100's on the 1:05. Unfortunately, the rest of the workout made that set look easy. I should have known it was going to be a tough one when Coach Tanner said he had a "fun" workout planned for us. Fun to watch, sure. Fun to swim? Not even close.

Six thousand yards later, both Brody and I were hanging on the wall, red-faced and trying to catch our breath.

"Great work, you two!" Coach Tanner cheered. He was standing on the pool deck looking down at us, clapping his hands. "I am very pleased with how you held all of those intervals the entire time. Go ahead and cool down, and then enjoy the rest of your afternoon. I'll be in my office if you need me." He disappeared into his office a minute later, leaving me alone with Brody once more.

I took a moment to catch my breath and then went right into my cool down. After spending the entire workout thinking about Brody, I decided I needed to talk to him and figure out exactly what he meant. If he wanted to be friends, then great. But if he wanted more, I'd have to put a stop to it.

When I finished my cool down, I climbed out of the water and procrastinated by slowly picking up my equipment and taking it to my bag. I still didn't have a clear idea of what I wanted to say to him, but suddenly, my mom's words from last night popped back into my head: *don't turn someone away who may be genuinely interested*. What if Brody really did want a relationship with me? Would I be making a mistake by telling him I only wanted to be friends? I was torn. My heart said I wasn't ready, but my gut was starting to think otherwise.

"Are you adjusting to the Florida climate?" Brody said from the bench next to mine. His question broke through my thoughts and I was thankful for the change of subject.

I nodded. "It's definitely hotter here, but I'm sure the warm winters will be a nice change from what I'm used to in Minnesota."

"What was it like growing up in Minnesota? Did you live there your whole life?"

"Yep, born and raised. My parents are farmers, our land is near Marshall, Minnesota. It's a small town, but we had everything we needed."

"Any siblings?" He wrapped his towel around his waist and took a seat on the bench. He patted the spot next to him, inviting me to take a seat beside him.

Smiling, I followed suit. "I have one sister, Mandy. She's a few years older than me, and married my brother-in-law, Paul, about two years ago. She's still in Minnesota, and lives in Rochester working for an insurance company."

"Were you two close?" He scooted closer to me so that our knees were touching.

I felt my face flush red. Keeping my gaze down so he wouldn't see, I cleared my throat before I continued. "Of course, she's my best friend. This is the farthest I've ever been away from her, but we both know how important swimming is to me. She already promised to come visit sometime."

"That's great." He flashed a smile so big I could see all of his teeth. "Family is so important."

"Absolutely," I agreed. "What about you? What's your story?"

The smile disappeared, and I immediately regretted asking. Coach Tanner told me the other day his parents had passed away, maybe his childhood wasn't something he liked to talk about.

He ran his hand over the back of his neck as he thought of a good response. After a moment, he simply shrugged. "Nothing too exciting to share. I'm an only child. Lived in Jacksonville my whole life, signed a swimming contract right out of high school. Started getting endorsements and sponsors only a few months into my career, so I've been living pretty good ever since—"

He stopped talking and stared wide-eyed at his feet. I waited a moment to see if he would continue.

"Ever since what?" I said finally.

He shook his head, shaking himself out of his trance. "Nothing, never mind." He stood up and grabbed his bag. "I should probably get going."

"Brody," I said before he could walk away. "Coach Tanner told me about your parents. If you ever want to talk about it, I'm here."

He shot me a brief smile. "Thanks. See you tomorrow?"

"Sure." I nodded. "See you later."

I watched him walk away and disappear into the locker room. Although I didn't get the answers I was looking for, that was okay. Friends get to know each other. Brody and I were friends, and that's all we will ever be. Nothing more.

So, why did it feel like I was trying so hard to convince myself of that?

Chapter Seven

Brody

Charlie already knew about my parents.

Why—and when—did Coach Tanner tell her? Should I be worried that they were talking about me? Who knows what else he could have told her.

I should've been pissed, and normally, I would be. However, I was the furthest thing from angry right now. In fact, I almost felt relieved that she already knew. I came with a lot of emotional baggage, and so far, she was handling it like a champ. This could finally be the girl who breaks down my walls, and the scary thing was: I might let her.

Admittedly, I was only after a good time when I first laid eyes on her. But now, I wanted more. She was beautiful yes, but she was also funny, easy to talk to, and very kind. We only just met, and she already offered to be there for me if I wanted to talk about my parents. I'd never met someone like that before.

Maybe I should open up to her, and tell her what happened. If anything were to come of this, she'd find out eventually anyway, right? Maybe if I just told her now, rather than later down the road, it'd hurt less if she decided to leave. I just needed to rip the band-aid off and do it.

I could have easily spent the entire day thinking about Charlie, and what I should tell her about my parents, but the sight of several extra cars parked in Roman's driveway shot me back to reality. Parking my car in my usual spot on the street, I made my way to the front door. Was everyone here because of the breach? Did Roman even want me here today after what happened? I guess there was only one way to find out.

After ringing the doorbell, I waited patiently on the front step for either Roman or Camila to come answer the door. While I waited, I could hear several different voices coming from inside, some of them yelling. After a moment, I wasn't sure if anyone actually heard the doorbell ring, so I rang it again. The voices inside quieted for a moment, and I heard footsteps coming towards the door. It swung open a moment later and Roman appeared before me, looking like a frazzled mess. His dress shirt had the first few buttons unbuttoned, his tie and suit jacket were missing, and his hair looked like he had run his hands through it a few too many times.

"Oh, Brody, I almost forgot you were coming," he said when he noticed it was me.

"I can come back at a better time?" I tried to peek around him to see what was going on inside, but he took a step to the side to block my view.

"No, you can come in. I sent my maids out for the day so I could conduct business from here. There's plenty of work for you to do." He ushered me inside behind him. He led me to the kitchen where half a dozen men wearing dark suits stood gathered around the island countertop. "Gentlemen," he addressed them. "I'll be back in a moment. Please wait to continue until I am back."

He then led me up the stairs to the third floor. "I need you to mop and vacuum all the floors up here on the third level, and then do the same for the second level. You can wait on doing the main floor for now. All the cleaning materials you need are in that closet over there." He pointed to a small door on the far side of the room.

"You want me to do the bedrooms as well?" I asked. "I don't want to upset Camila like I did yesterday."

"Yes, do the bedrooms." He started walking back down the stairs as he spoke. "Camila isn't here. I haven't seen her since this morning. She probably went shopping or something."

"You don't know where she is?" I asked.

"She's an adult!" he barked from halfway down the stairs. "She slips off to God knows where all the time. I don't have time to track her down right now."

I tried to remember if she ever disappeared while we were together, but couldn't recall any such times. That was certainly strange. Roman was probably right though. She probably just went off to do some shopping and didn't bother to tell anyone.

I went to the cleaning closet and pulled out the vacuum, then went to the first bedroom to the left and opened the door to go inside. When I switched on the light, I saw the largest bedroom I had ever been in. This room itself was probably the same size as the main floor of my house. There was a massive king-size bed on the far side, and there had to be at least three full-sized walk-in closets filled to the brim with garments of all shapes and sizes.

This must be Roman and Camila's room.

And this room alone was going to take me forever to vacuum. Not to mention the massive bathroom that would need mopping. No wonder they hired so many people to clean for them. I sighed and got to work.

I had only been vacuuming for a few minutes before realizing this was going to take a lot longer than I originally thought. Not only because the room was massive, but because there were several articles of clothing, shoes, handbags, and other pieces of junk thrown about the room that I had to pick up. Eventually, I decided it would be easier to turn the vacuum off, and pick everything up off the floor before starting again.

Hopefully Roman's maids were being paid very well for this job, because this was driving me insane.

As I was bending down to grab a pair of Camila's heels, I heard my phone ping. I took it from my pocket and saw a text message from Landon.

Landon: Hey, I think I'll be okay to stay at my dad's tonight. He's been in a super good mood today. He told me he'd take me to practice tonight and pick me up. He even took me out to pizza for lunch.

I wondered what had gotten Mr. Davis in such a good mood. He rarely spent time with Landon. But people can change. Maybe he was going to start making more of an effort.

Me: Glad to hear it, man! You're still welcome to come over if something changes.

Before sliding my phone back into my pocket, I attempted to send Chase *another* text asking him where he's been. I hadn't heard or seen him since Friday night, and it was pissing me off. If he didn't respond by the time I was done here, I would stop by his house on the way home.

I went back to picking up all the junk littering the floor, and before long I was able to start vacuuming again. After a while, I found myself zoning out. My mind was buzzing along with the sound of the vacuum cleaner, and my movements became more automatic. I was so out of it, that when I lifted the bed skirt on the mattress to vacuum under the bed, I hit something hard a couple of times before I thought to turn off the machine and investigate.

Getting on my hands and knees, I reached a hand under the bed to search for what I had hit. A moment later, I grabbed onto something cold and metal, and my eyes bulged when I realized what it was.

A gun.

The item itself didn't surprise me. Roman was one of the richest men in Florida, and it wasn't a secret. If I flaunted my money like that, I'd probably need a gun to protect myself, too.

But why did he have it under their bed? Surely, Roman could afford a gun safe. Turning the gun over in my hands, I realized the safety wasn't on, and there were several rounds in the magazine. Had it been used recently? On who, and for what reason? Regardless, keeping the gun there in that condition was an accident waiting to happen.

Clicking on the safety, I emptied the clip and set both that and the gun itself on one of the nightstands. I thought about taking it downstairs and showing Roman right away, but decided to wait until the suits left and things settled down a little bit. I didn't need to make a scene when tensions were already running high.

I went back to work, and by the time I finally finished Roman and Camila's bedroom, it was nearly 5:30. Dragging the vacuum and the mop bucket back out into the hallway, I listened for voices downstairs, but didn't hear any. In need of a break anyway, I made my way to the kitchen to tell Roman about the gun.

Downstairs, I found Roman sitting alone at the kitchen table. He was staring wide-eyed at his open laptop, and his hair was even more disheveled than before.

I cleared my throat before speaking in case he didn't hear me approach. "Roman?"

He looked up from his computer. "Are you finished?"

"No, but I wanted to let you know that I found a gun under your bed," I said. "The safety was off and a magazine clip full of rounds was in it. Is there a safer place I can put it for you?"

A puzzled look crossed his face. "A gun?"

"Yeah, the one in your bedroom. I think it was a .22 pistol."

He shook his head. "Brody, I don't own a gun."

"You don't?"

"No, I have a state-of-the-art security system. Why would I need a gun?" He went back to looking at his laptop.

Not about to have that argument with him, I took a few steps further into the room. "Roman, I still found a gun in your room," I repeated. "If you don't own a gun, then who's is it? Does Camila have one?"

His brows furrowed. "I don't think she does."

Dread began to creep up my spine. "So, doesn't that kind of concern you?"

He stared straight ahead and chewed on his lip as he thought about it. Finally, his gaze met mine again. "I suppose that is kind of strange, isn't it?"

"Do you have cameras inside?" I asked him. "Maybe you should find out who's been upstairs."

He nodded and held up his pointer finger. "Yeah, that's a good idea." He began typing on his computer. "It'll just take a second to pull it up."

Suddenly, the front door swung open and slammed shut a moment later. The sounds of footsteps pounding along the rug in the entryway followed. "Roman?" Camila called.

"We're in the kitchen, darling," he called back to her without looking up from his computer.

A moment later, she came sashaying into the kitchen, dressed in a skin-tight black dress with matching black pumps. Her blonde hair was curled and bounced lightly as she walked. "What are you doing in here?"

Roman gave her a quick kiss when she stopped next to him. "We're checking the security cameras. Brody found a gun in our bedroom while he was cleaning."

"What?" Camila's head snapped up in shock. "Our bedroom? Why were you in our bedroom?" Her icy gaze landed on me.

"I gave him permission to," Roman assured her. "Someone had to clean up the mess you made. Don't worry, we'll get to the bottom of this."

"Roman, you know how many of your maids go up and down these halls during the day? It could have been anyone." Camila's words came out a mile a minute, and her voice shook as though she were nervous. "And how do you even know the gun was left in there today? Who knows how long it's been under there."

"How'd you know it was under anything?" I asked Camila. "Roman didn't say where it was. He said I found it in the bedroom."

Camila froze to her spot with her mouth hanging open as though she were trying to think of something to say.

"That's a good point," Roman added. He turned away from his computer and took Camila's hands in his. "Honey, do you have something you'd like to tell me? Is the gun yours?"

She hesitated for a moment, and then sighed. "Yes, the gun is mine."

"Why didn't you tell me you had a gun?"

"I didn't want you to worry," she pouted. "I thought maybe we could use the extra protection."

"Do you even know how to use it?" I choked out a laugh. "The safety wasn't on, it was full of ammo, and it was just lying around."

She glared at me. "Brody, I don't think this concerns you."

"If it wasn't for him, I wouldn't know there was a gun in our bedroom," Roman said, turning back to his computer. "At least now I know who it belongs to. Don't you worry, honey. We are perfectly safe. But since I have the security footage up already, I might just take a look through it."

"Roman, honey, I'm hungry." Camila reached across him and closed his laptop. "Let's go out for dinner tonight!"

"Camila, I was using that." Roman turned to her and frowned. "How many times do I have to tell you that it bothers me when you do that."

"Oops!" She squealed, shrugging her shoulders. "Let's go eat." She took his hand in hers and attempted to pull him out of his seat.

Roman let out a long sigh. "Alright, fine. Brody, you can be finished for this evening."

"That's it?" I said in disbelief. "You're not even going to ask her anything else about the gun? Like why it was loaded and ready to shoot—?"

"Brody." Roman held his hand up to stop me. "I appreciate that you brought the situation to my attention. But now I have to agree with Camila: it doesn't concern you anymore. The two of us will talk about it."

"Are you also going to talk about the fact that she disappeared the day you discovered a breach at your company? That's probably something worth talking about, too. But what do I know, right?" I don't know why I suddenly felt so irritated, but I was. It was frustrating to watch Camila walk all over Roman, and from my viewpoint, something seemed off. He didn't seem to notice, though.

"That's quite enough, Brody." Roman stood from his chair. "Now, I'm not asking. You may show yourself out."

My eyes locked with Camila's. Her eyes were ablaze with anger, and I swore she was grinding her teeth behind her pouted lips.

Without another word, I left the kitchen and exited the house. I suddenly wished I had another swim practice tonight in order to work off some of this frustration.

Maybe it shouldn't have bothered me so much, but it did. Something weird was going on, whether Roman wanted to listen or not, and I was going to find out what it was.

******

Since Chase still hadn't responded to any of my messages by the time I left Roman's house, I decided it was time to pay him a visit. He could only avoid me for so long, and he had some explaining to do.

Chase still lived in his parents' basement, and pulling up to their house always brought up a ton of memories from growing up together. Typically, I enjoyed remembering all the good times we had, but I was still in a bad mood from earlier and didn't feel like reminiscing today. After parking behind his car in the driveway, I stomped up his front step and slammed my fist on the door several times. When I heard footsteps on the other side, I hoped it was Chase and not his parents. There was a brief pause before the door opened, but when it did, Chase smiled at me like there was nothing wrong.

"Brody! How's it hanging, my friend?" His long hair hung low to his shoulders, and he looked and smelled as though he had been wearing the same t-shirt and sweat pants for the last few days. "Do you want to come in?"

Crossing my arms, I narrowed my eyes at him. "No, I don't want to come in. You owe me an explanation, Chase. What the hell were you thinking last week?"

His smile faded immediately. "Look, I know you're mad at me—"

"No shit I'm mad at you!" I yelled back. "You let me take the blame for what you did."

"I know, I'm not really sure what came over me." He rubbed the back of his head with his hand. "You were telling me about what Camila said, and then when we saw her, I just felt like I had to get back at her somehow."

"I don't need you to fight my battles for me."

"Isn't that what friends do for one another?" he asked.

"Friends don't smash other people's cars and then leave said friend behind. And why haven't you been answering your phone? I've called you and texted you a million times."

He shrugged. "I've been busy."

I glanced past him where I had a view of the stairs that lead to the basement. His Xbox was so loud, I could hear the *Call of Duty* game he had playing from here. "Sounds like you've been busy."

He suddenly became defensive. "Honestly, you should be thanking me for having the guts to do what you've wanted to do for months. She broke your heart when she cheated on you. It's only fair that you break something of hers."

I was so angry, I was seeing red. "That's not how that works, Chase. We broke up, that was that. I didn't need to get revenge. But now you've got everyone thinking that's what I was doing."

"Good!" he snorted. "You're welcome. *Again.*"

"Oh, my God." I shook my head. "I can't deal with this anymore. We're done hanging out, Chase. I can't be seen with you anymore. Consider this friendship over." I turned and started stomping my way back to my car.

"Hold up!" he called after me. "That's it? You're just going to cut me out of your life?"

Turning around to face him, I nodded. "Coach Tanner was right: I should have done it a long time ago." I continued walking and didn't turn back.

"Well, fuck you, man!" he yelled.

From my truck, I saw him flipping me off with both hands. He was still yelling, but I turned up my radio and it drowned him out.

As I drove away, I felt as though a giant weight had been lifted off my shoulders. I knew at some point I'd have to cut Chase out of my life, and the way he reacted to me being there today made it so much easier than I thought it would be.

Now, if I made a stupid decision, I had no one to blame but myself. And now that the bad influencer was out of my life, I was certain it would be a long time before I found myself in another sticky situation.

Boy, was I wrong.

Chapter Eight

Charlie

Early the following morning, I decided to treat myself to breakfast before practice. Luckily, there was a small coffee shop down the street from the pool that was open early enough for me to stop by and sit down.

Sipping on a latte and munching on a breakfast sandwich, I took a few minutes to scroll through current job openings in Jacksonville. My job search wasn't off to a great start, but I was constantly looking through the list of openings in hopes something amazing would come along.

I was reading through a job description for a manager at a local grocery store, when I sensed someone approaching my table.

"Is this seat taken?"

I looked up and saw Brody staring back down at me with a cup of coffee in his hand. Shaking my head, I motioned for him to take a seat.

"I see you've found one of Jacksonville's hidden treasures." He smiled. "I like to come here before practice every now and again. It's a nice, quiet little spot to hang out. Plus, their lattes are easily the best I've ever had."

Raising my latte to his, we clinked cups. "I second that. I'll certainly be coming back for more."

He took a deep breath. "So, I'm glad I ran into you. I was hoping I'd get a chance to talk to you about what happened last night and apologize for leaving so abruptly."

"No, Brody, there's no reason for you to apologize. If I said anything to upset you—"

He held up his hand to stop me. "You didn't say anything wrong. It just caught me off guard. I didn't know you knew about my parents."

"Coach Tanner might have mentioned something about it the other day." I pressed my lips into a straight line and shrugged.

"It's not something I really like to talk about. My life really changed after that, and I haven't been the same since."

"How could you be? I can't imagine what my life would be like if my parents were gone."

"Well, since you already know." He looked down at the ground while he spoke. "I also want you to know that I have a really hard time letting people in. It's not because I don't like you, it's because I'm ..." he stopped, as if he couldn't find the right words to say.

"Because you're afraid," I finished for him. "You're afraid of losing someone again."

"You could say that," he said quietly. "I don't like to admit that. It makes me look weak."

"Brody, you lost your parents. It would be crazy for you *not* to feel the way you do."

"I suppose you're right." He nodded. "But for some reason, it tends to scare some people away. Like somehow *my* emotional damage is a burden for *them*."

"Well, it's not going to scare me away." I reached a hand across the table and placed it on his.

He stared at my hand for a moment and met my gaze. His eyes softened, and if I wasn't mistaken, it looked as though his shoulders relaxed too, as if he had been holding his breath in anticipation. "Thank you," he breathed. "It actually means a lot to hear you say that."

I smiled. "Of course."

He then sat up and leaned across the table as though he were going to kiss me. Instinctively, my eyes widened in surprise, and my whole body went still as I waited to see what he would do next.

Reaching towards me, he tucked a loose strand of hair behind my ear. "I have a good feeling about you, Charlie," he whispered.

"You do?" My heart was beating so loud, I was certain he could hear it.

"Yeah," he smiled, showing me all his teeth. "I'm excited to see where this goes."

I swallowed the lump in my throat as he sat back in his chair. A part of me felt relieved, and another part of me was left wishing he *had* kissed me.

Shaking the thought from my head, I checked the time on my phone. "We should probably get going, we don't want to be late." I gathered up all my things in a hurry and avoided Brody's gaze as he got up and followed me out the door.

We walked to the pool together in a comfortable silence. Neither of us said anything, but it didn't really feel like we had to. We were enjoying each other's presence, and that was all we needed. He held the door open for me when we arrived at the pool, and I mumbled a thank you under my breath.

"I'll see you out there," he finally said when we had reached the locker rooms. "We should do this again sometime."

I nodded and disappeared into the women's locker room. Almost certain I was blushing, I didn't want him to see my face. Then when I was finally alone with my thoughts, I mentally kicked myself for getting caught up in the moment and not being honest with him. I needed to tell him I only wanted to be friends, but for some reason, I couldn't get the words to leave my mouth. The longer I waited, the harder it would be.

Before long, we were in the water and well into our workout. It didn't take me long to realize I was thinking about Brody more than I was focusing on my set. I had to ask Coach Tanner to repeat himself twice, and missed an interval that should have been easily doable.

By the end, I was able to get myself back on track and my head in the game, but I felt guilty for not being totally present for the entire practice. I did a longer cool down in an attempt to make up for it, and then finally pulled myself out of the water to get ready for the lifting session.

"Charlie, where was your head at this morning?" Coach Tanner asked when I was standing on the pool deck.

"I'm sorry, Coach, that was definitely not my best effort," I said as I wrung the water out of my hair.

"I agree. Get it together, Price. It's still your first week, don't be slacking on me already."

"I know." I hung my head in shame. "It won't happen again."

"Better not. You've worked too hard for this." He gave me a pat on the shoulder. "Now, go get changed for the lifting session."

I kept my gaze on the floor as I made my way to the locker room. Embarrassed and upset with myself, I was quiet while I changed, and during our next workout. It was only my third day as a professional swimmer, and I was letting a boy get in my head and distract me from what I was here to do. Maybe I needed to keep Brody at arm's length for a while. I wasn't even looking for a relationship, and the thought of a boy potentially wanting one with me was distracting me from my dream.

Coach Tanner was right: I worked too hard for this. I didn't need any distractions right now.

When the lifting session was over, Brody came my way with a big smile on his face, and I prepared myself for what I would have to tell him.

"Hey, you want to get lunch?" he asked. "We've worked up an appetite this morning. It'll be my treat."

Giving him a tight smile, I shook my head. "I can't, Allison and I are getting lunch today."

"Okay, what about tomorrow?"

"I have a thing. I actually think I have a thing every day this week."

His smile disappeared and he narrowed his eyes. "I'm getting the feeling that you just don't want to go."

I looked away from Brody, not wanting to meet his gaze. "I don't think it would be a good idea right now."

"Getting lunch?"

"Us hanging out outside of practice."

He cursed under his breath. "I knew it. I knew if I told you about my past, you'd get freaked out. You promised you wouldn't."

Snapping my gaze back to Brody, I realized how this looked to him. "No, it's not that. I don't need—"

"Save it," he spat. "I don't need your excuses." He turned towards the locker room without another word.

"Brody!" I called to him, but he ignored me.

"Everything okay?" Allison asked when she reached my side.

"How much of that did you hear?" I hadn't realized she had been standing close by.

"Enough." She shrugged. "You want to talk about it?"

I sighed. "I don't know."

"Well, are you still free for lunch? If you feel like talking about it, we can. If you don't, then we won't."

"Sure, let's get changed and go," I told her. I could use the distraction anyway.

Once we had quickly cleaned up and made ourselves presentable, we made the short walk over to a local diner. It was dreadfully hot out already, with little cloud coverage to offer us relief. Regardless of the athletic shorts and tank top I was wearing, I was still breaking a sweat. Thankfully, it only took a few minutes to walk to the diner, and the air conditioning inside felt delightful.

It was a little hole-in-the-wall restaurant squeezed between two other businesses, and I likely would have missed it if Allison hadn't pointed it out. The outside was covered in old bricks, and the inside was dimly lit and smelled faintly of cigar smoke. It was clear the place hadn't been renovated in a while, as many of the chairs and booths had rips in them held together with duct tape, and the tables were lopsided and wobbly.

"So, I know this place looks a little run down," Allison whispered after we had been seated in a small booth by a short, plump waitress. "But I promise you the food makes up for the atmosphere."

"I'm so hungry, I'll take anything at this point." I smiled and opened the menu. They had everything from breakfast food to burgers, sandwiches to pasta, and seafood. If I didn't already have a craving for a burger and fries, it would have been a difficult decision. Our waitress returned a few minutes later with some iced water and took our order.

"So, I want to know how your first week is going," Allison said after the waitress took our menus and walked away. "Is it what you expected it to be like? Give me the details."

"It's going well so far, although I'm surprised I can still move," I joked. "I've been taking ice baths every night this week, but I'm still pretty sore."

"Were you able to get an appointment for a massage? It really would make a huge difference."

"Not yet, but it's definitely on my agenda."

She smiled. "How is everything otherwise? Are you settled in? I'm happy to help where I can."

"For the most part, I am. I still need to find a job, though. That's what I've been doing this week when I haven't been at the pool."

"What kind of work are you looking for? I might be able to point you in the right direction."

"I studied business in school, and I'd really like to be a manager somewhere. I'm not picky, whether it be in a restaurant, or some other small business that has part-time work available to accommodate my swimming schedule."

"You know, I think you might be in luck!" A huge grin spread across her face. "Remember the other day when I told you I worked at another gym? They've had a management position open for a few weeks now. I could put in a good word for you this afternoon when I get to work. The pay is decent, and Landon's dad actually owns the place, so he's good about working around my swimming schedule. I'm sure he would do the same for you."

"Oh, wow. What a small world." I smiled. "That's got to be nice to work for someone you know."

She made a face. "Actually Mr. Davis is probably the only thing I don't like about that job. He's got a bit of a temper problem. But as long as he stays out of my way and I stay out of his, it works out. Plus, I'm not in a position to be super picky."

"Yikes." I grimaced. "I wonder how Landon handles that."

"Brody hasn't told you?" she asked.

I frowned, confused. "Told me what?"

She shook her head. "Sorry, I don't know why I assumed that was something you guys would talk about. Landon doesn't have the best home life. He and his dad don't really get along, so he doesn't spend a lot of time at home."

"Oh?"

Before Allison could continue, the waitress was back with our food. She set down my plate in front of me, and my mouth started to water. The burger looked delicious with cheese oozing out the side, and steam rolling off the top. Allison had ordered the mac and cheese, and the waitress delivered the largest plate of mac and cheese I think I had ever seen. From the look on Allison's face, I could tell she was just as hungry as I was.

"Anyway," Allison continued after taking a few bites of her pasta. "Landon's mom died when he was little, and he was raised by his dad. Mr. Davis comes to all of Landon's meets, but he seems to put an unnecessary amount of pressure on him. He's convinced Landon will be a shoo-in for the next Olympics—which is very possible since we're all training for it. But, Landon's still young. He's only seventeen, he has plenty of time and I don't think his dad realizes that.

"One time, after Landon swam the 100 freestyle, he was seeded to win his heat, but he came in fourth instead. His dad was furious and started yelling at him, and I swear if we hadn't been nearby, his dad would have really lost it. I know it's a strong accusation, but I think his dad hits him. Like that bruise he's got on his eye? I'd bet money his dad did that. I asked Brody about it, but he told me to drop it."

"That's awful," I said quietly.

"Isn't it?" Her voice was laced with frustration. "Like, who does that to their kid? And poor Landon. It's not like he can just leave. Mr. Davis has legal guardianship over him for a few more months until he's eighteen, and Landon would never say anything to get him in trouble. He's too nice of a kid. Thankfully, Brody lets Landon stay at his house whenever he wants. Those two have become really close."

"Brody looks after Landon?" I asked, trying to keep the surprise out of my voice.

Allison nodded, swallowing a large mouthful of pasta. "Oh yeah, he's like the big brother Landon never had. It really is very sweet of him. Of course, he'd never admit it himself, but Brody is kind of a softy. Once you break through that shell of his, there's very little he wouldn't do for you."

I chewed silently for a moment while I processed what she said. This was definitely new information to me.

"Anyway, back to the job," Allison said. "I'd be more than happy to put a good word in for you. If you get the management position, it's very likely Mr. Davis won't be around much while you're on shift, anyway."

"Please do." I nodded. "That would be so helpful." My shoulders sagged with relief. Obviously, nothing was set in stone, but this would be perfect. "You have no idea how much stress that would take off my shoulders."

"Trust me, I get it. I also struggled to find work that would bring in a good income while maintaining a swimming career. I was in the same boat only a few years ago. Although, I'm from Miami, so I didn't have to add moving across the country to my pile of stress. If there's anything I can help with at all, please let me know. We're here to look out for each other."

"You're awesome, I can't tell you how much I appreciate that."

She laughed. "It's no problem at all."

We fell silent for a while as we continued to eat our food. Eventually, I decided I just needed to come out and tell her about what's been going on between Brody and me.

"So, if I tell you something, do you promise not to tell anyone?" I wiped my mouth with my napkin and then folded my hands in my lap.

"Of course." She nodded. "Is everything okay?"

I let out a nervous chuckle. "I don't know. I'm really confused."

Over the next couple of minutes, I told her about my former relationship with Nick, and how I had sworn off any relationships for the near future. I told her about the interaction Brody and I had the first day we met, and everything that had happened since then.

"I'm definitely not ready for a relationship right now. I know I'm not," I continued. "But for some reason I can't get myself to tell him that, and I think I might be leading him on."

"If you can't get yourself to tell him, do you think it's because deep down you *do* want a relationship with him?" she asked. The tiniest hint of a smile played at the corners of her mouth.

"I don't know." I shook my head. "I feel like I'm trying really hard to convince myself that I don't."

"Well, if you're hoping I'll try and talk you out of it, then you've got another thing coming." She crossed her arms and sat back in her seat.

I couldn't help but laugh. "Why not?"

"Because Brody needs someone to keep him in line, and you seem like someone who wouldn't put up with his shit. And just because your last boyfriend ended up being a jerk, doesn't mean all guys are."

"I know, but it wasn't that long ago," I reminded her. "It still stings."

"And it's going to, but going after someone new might ease that pain and give you something better to look forward to."

"I guess, but what about my career?" I argued. "I came to Jacksonville to swim. To make a career out of the sport I love, not to chase boys."

"Who says you can't have both?"

"Coach Tanner pulled me aside this morning and told me I needed to get my head in the game. Brody is already becoming a distraction, and nothing has really happened yet. What if something does develop between us, and down the road, he leaves me for someone better? He's Brody Hayes, for Christ's sake. He can literally have any girl he wants. He'd get bored of me before too long, and I don't think I'd be able to handle that. I'd have to switch teams or something. My career could really take a hit."

She shook her head. "Charlie, you're overthinking this. You don't know what could come of it until you've given him a chance. I've known Brody for years. I won't lie to you, he's always had his fair share of attention from the ladies, but he's also grown up a lot since I first met him. He is capable of being in a relationship and giving his whole self to one girl. Have you met Roman yet? And Camila?"

"No, but I know who they are."

"Camila is Roman's assistant, and his girlfriend. Brody used to date her. They dated for quite a while, and he was really into her. He would have moved mountains for that woman. In the end, though, she screwed him over bad. I don't know the details, but I do know that he hasn't let anyone else get that close to him since."

"That doesn't make me feel any better—"

She held up a finger to stop me. "I'm not finished. I know for a fact that Brody is capable of being in a committed relationship, but it surprises me that you turned him down, and he keeps coming back. That's not like Brody. He's not going to waste his time pursuing someone who isn't interested."

"Well, I'm not sure he's going to keep trying after this morning."

"Do you want to tell me what happened?" she asked. She folded her hands on the table to show me I had her full attention.

I sighed. "When he told me about his parents, he told me that it tends to scare some women away because of the emotional baggage he carries, and that's why he hasn't been looking for an actual relationship for a while. I assured him it wouldn't scare me away, and that I completely understood his feelings on the matter."

She nodded in approval. "Good, I'm glad you said that."

"But then I ruined it. After Coach Tanner talked to me about my performance, I kind of freaked out. I didn't want a relationship to get in between me and my career. So, I told Brody that I didn't want to pursue anything, and he thought it was because of what he told me about his parents. He thinks I lied to him."

Allison grimaced. "Shoot. I can see where he'd think that."

"I wanted to explain it to him, but he left before I had the chance."

"Well, the good news is that you will have a chance to explain it to him tomorrow," she said. "If he doesn't listen, he'll have me to deal with." She winked.

I laughed but didn't say anything.

"But, if I could also add my two cents on the matter, I really do think you should give him a chance. He really is a great guy."

"I don't know, I'm still pretty hesitant to jump into a new relationship. What if things go south between us?"

"Then you worry about that when you get there. You're both adults. I think you can figure out a way to be civilized around each other for a few hours every day."

"Maybe." I played with my food for a moment before I looked back at Allison. She was wearing that huge grin on her face, and I couldn't help but smile back. "Alright, fine. I'll talk to him and see where it goes from there."

"Yay!" She threw her hands up and did a little happy dance in her seat. "You're making the right choice, Charlie. I don't think you'll regret it."

I sure hoped she was right.

Chapter Nine

Brody

By the time I arrived at the pool Thursday morning and changed into my suit, I still had twenty minutes before practice started and I was the only one on deck. I was secretly hoping Charlie wouldn't show up until right before practice so I wouldn't have to speak to her before then. After the conversation with her yesterday, I had no desire to talk to her. She lied to me after she promised she wouldn't. I couldn't forgive her that easily.

Unfortunately, even though I was upset with her, I still couldn't get the girl off my mind. No matter how hard I tried, she just kept creeping her way back into my thoughts. It didn't help that I spent all yesterday afternoon on my own. Mike had called and told me they had enough photos, so no photoshoot; and while I did end up mowing the lawn and trimming some branches at Roman's house, somehow my mind kept creeping back to Charlie. As much as I didn't want to admit it, she had left a mark on me.

As if she knew I was thinking about her, Charlie came out of the locker room a minute later dressed in a bright pink one-piece suit. She turned her back to me to set her bag down on a bench, and I caught my gaze wandering down to her ass again. The way her suit was hugging all of her curves so tightly nearly made my mouth water.

She was breathtakingly beautiful.

Stop thinking about her.

Shaking myself out of my trance, I went to turn away, but was a moment too slow. She turned around and our gazes met immediately. I looked away quickly, but only for a moment. I couldn't stop myself from looking back at her.

The faintest of smiles appeared on her lips, and she made her way over to me. I wanted to make myself look busy to let her know I didn't want to talk to her, but couldn't get myself to do it.

"Good morning," she said when she had reached me.

"Hey," I said quietly.

"I owe you an explanation."

I nodded.

"I didn't lie to you," she started. "I was scared a relationship would interfere with my career. I had a little bit of trouble focusing during the morning workout yesterday and I panicked. I didn't think things through before I talked to you, and I realized too late how that looked from your perspective. The last thing I want is for you to think your family history affected that decision."

My spirits raised, but only slightly. "I'm really glad you told me that. I appreciate it."

"Of course." She gave me a tight smile.

"Is your decision still the same?" I braved the question. "You still don't want to see where this could go?"

She shrugged. "I don't know. I've worked really hard to get here. I like you, Brody, but I can't let a relationship affect my career."

"I totally get that. And it will take work, but I think we could do it. I'm not going to stop trying to convince you to give me a chance. I can't explain the way I feel, but it's like I'm being drawn to you. You're always on my mind, even when I don't want you to be."

She blushed. "You've been on my mind, too."

"So, what do you think? Can we give this a try? I promise you won't regret it."

"What if I do regret it?" she teased. "What will you do then?"

"Whatever you want me to." I smiled.

She laughed. "Okay, let's give this a shot."

My face lit up, and I breathed a sigh of relief. "So, how about I try this again. Do you want to have lunch with me today? We could go after the lifting session and come back together for the afternoon workout."

"That sounds perfect," she said. She tucked a loose piece of her hair behind her ear and stared at her feet as if she were suddenly shy.

She was adorable.

I reached forward and placed a hand on her cheek, forcing her to look back at me. "Thank you for giving me a chance. I'm really excited to see where this goes."

Her face blushed a deeper shade of red. She opened her mouth to respond but shut it quickly when the clicking of heels sounded on the pavement behind us.

"Well, what do we have going on here?" Came a shrill, female voice.

I didn't even have to look to know who was standing next to us.

"Camila," I said, dropping my hand from Charlie's face. Charlie turned to face her.

"Hello, Brody. Long time, no see." She smirked.

She then turned her attention to Charlie, and her face suddenly darkened. She scowled and looked at her like she was vermin. Charlie's eyes darted between Camila and me, clearly trying to read each of our expressions.

Before any of us could say anything more, Coach Tanner came bounding out of his office. "Camila! What a surprise. To what do we owe this pleasure?"

"Oh, Coach Tanner, Roman and I wanted to meet your new swimmer of course," she said as she disregarded Charlie and me, and moved past us. The pale blue pencil skirt she was wearing made it look as though she were having a difficult time walking— either that, or it was the four-inch white heels that clicked along the pool deck as she went.

"Of course." Coach stopped her when she reached him and turned her around to face Charlie once more. "Camila, this is Charlie Price. She just moved here from Minnesota. Charlie, this is Camila Hale. She is Roman Howard's assistant. Roman Howard is the CEO and founder of Howard Enterprises. He is one of our most valued sponsors, as I have mentioned to you before."

"Of course, nice to finally meet you." Charlie held her hand out to shake Camila's.

"Believe me, the pleasure is mine." Camila gave her a tight smile but ignored her outstretched hand.

The side door of the pool opened a moment later, and Roman came bursting in, talking on his cell phone. "Yes, that'll be all for now," he said into the phone. "I need to go, I'll call again this afternoon to finalize the details … yes, I'm about to talk to him now … sounds good, bye."

"Roman, it's a delight to see you this morning." Coach Tanner reached out to shake his hand. "Camila was telling us that you were interested in meeting our new swimmer."

"Yes, of course. It's great to meet you," he said, shaking Charlie's hand. "I also came because I wanted to make up for the lost funds that were supposed to be for your swim meet this weekend." Roman started scrolling through his phone, seemingly distracted by whatever he was looking at.

"Roman, that's quite alright," Coach said. "You have bigger fish to fry right now."

"Nonsense." He waved his hand, dismissing Coach's comment. "I always keep my promises, and if for some reason I can't, I make up for it. Now, it is a little short notice, and for that I do apologize, but I have gone ahead and set up a swim clinic this weekend for youth swimmers. You can then keep the funds we raise for future swim meets. How does that sound?"

"Oh, that's wonderful," Coach said with fake enthusiasm. By the tone of his voice, it wasn't what he had expected. "I suspect you will be needing my swimmers to help at this camp?"

"Yes, I will." Roman didn't look up as he continued to pound the keys on his phone. "I'll need you to be there as well to help keep everything together. I'm assuming none of you have anything going on? You were going to have a swim meet, after all."

I stifled a groan. Of course, Roman would think replacing a swim meet with a swim clinic would be the appropriate thing to do. We wanted to race, not babysit a bunch of kids.

Coach Tanner turned to Charlie and me, "Are you two available to help at this swim clinic?"

We both nodded.

"What exactly would we be doing?" Charlie asked.

"You'd be teaching the kids to swim of course," Camila quickly answered, sounding a little annoyed with the question. "What do you think you would do at a swim clinic?"

"Duties often vary. That's why I'm asking." Charlie looked to Coach, and then to me for help.

"Don't worry, Charlie," Coach Tanner patted her shoulder reassuringly. "I'm sure Roman has everything set to go for this clinic, and Camila will be sending us an itinerary by the end of the day. Isn't that right, Camila?"

"Yeah, sure." She waved her hand dismissively. "Can you handle something like this, sweetie?" She said to Charlie.

What was her problem today?

"I think I can manage." Charlie pursed her lips. She turned and walked away from us before anyone could say anything else.

"Take it easy on her, Camila." Coach sounded impatient. "She's new."

"Regardless, I'm a little concerned that she didn't know what to do at a swim clinic. I mean, *come on!*" She snickered as if Charlie wasn't standing only a few feet away.

"Do *you* even know what to do at a swim clinic, Camila?" I threw at her.

"Of course. Don't be silly, Brody," she snickered. "But, I don't need to waste any of your time explaining it. I'm sure Tanner here would like to get your practice started."

"I would, actually." Coach Tanner was trying to hide a smirk. "Thank you, Camila."

Roman's phone rang again, and he turned away from us to answer it. "This is Roman … now's a great time. Talk to me."

"Oh, Tanner," Camila said sweetly before Coach could walk off. "Would you mind if I had a private word with Brody? It will only take a moment."

Coach stole a quick glance in my direction before he answered her. "I trust this is important? You know how crucial these workouts are for my swimmers."

"Of course. I just need to discuss Brody's chores for next week."

"Alright then," Coach Tanner said as he walked away. "Everyone else, we are getting in the water in two minutes." He wandered over to Allison and Landon, who had come out on deck sometime while we had been talking to Camila. I overheard him mention the swim clinic to them before turning to Camila.

"Can't you just tell me what chores I have when I show up like you have been?" I asked her, slightly annoyed that I was going to be late getting in the water.

"Oh hush," she snapped. "That's not what I wanted to talk to you about. We need to talk about that girl."

"Charlie? What about her?"

"I saw you two getting cozy earlier, and I don't like it." She crossed her arms over her chest and stuck her nose in the air. "You want Roman's funding, you'll put an end to it, now."

I laughed. "You and I both know you don't have *that* much control over his financial decisions."

"You'd be surprised what I'm capable of, Brody," she snarled.

"Why does it bother you, anyway? You've moved on. I have too. In your own words: 'I'm no longer your concern.'"

"I don't like her," she pouted. She traced one of her fingers lightly up and down my bicep. "I know you, Brody. You deserve so much better."

I took a step back so that I was out of her reach. "You don't know me, Camila, and given our past, you're the last person I would trust to give me advice on my love life."

"Love life?" Her mouth dropped open in surprise. "Brody, you barely know her."

"I don't care. Regardless, it doesn't concern you. I'm done with this conversation." I turned to leave.

She grabbed my arm and held me in place. "Brody, I'm not finished."

"Well, I said I was." I jerked out of her hold and walked away from her before I could say what was really on my mind.

"Brody!" She yelled after me.

I didn't respond. I just kept walking towards the pool, pulling my goggles over my head as I went.

"Is everything okay?" Coach Tanner asked as I stormed by.

"Just fine." I jumped in the pool before he could say anything else.

******

After a grueling practice of way too many 100 sprints, I clung to the side of the pool, trying to catch my breath. I had taken all of my frustration with Camila out on the water for the last few hours, and I felt a little less angry than I had before.

How dare Camila come here and claim she knows what's best for me. Who the hell did she think she was? And why on earth did she even care? We had been over for a long time now. It was no longer her concern who I was seeing.

"Hey, what did Camila want?" Allison asked when I had pulled myself out of the water. "You looked like you were ready to kill someone after you talked to her."

"That's because I was," I laughed. "She's just trying to butt her nose into my personal life. I told her it wasn't any of her concern."

"Good! I'm so sick of her thinking she still has some kind of hold over you," she said. "Honestly, I know she's pretty, but what did you ever see in her?"

"That's a good question. Not sure I could tell you."

"Well, let me know if I need to slap a bitch." She winked. "I've got your back."

Laughing again, I shook my head. "Thanks, Allison. Appreciate it."

"By the way," she whispered, leaning in closer. "Charlie told me you two have a date this afternoon."

I couldn't hold back my smile. "She told you that, huh?"

"Yes! Now, *she's* a catch, Brody. You better not hurt her though. I'd hate to have to choose sides."

"I wouldn't dream of hurting her."

Chapter Ten

Charlie

Throughout the lifting session, I listened to Allison go on and on about how excited she was that Brody and I were going on a date this afternoon. At this point, she was probably more thrilled than I was.

"This is just so exciting!" she squealed after another long tangent of how cute we were together. "He's had such a rough couple of years. He deserves someone like you to come into his life and sweeten things up a bit."

"It's just one date," I told her for what felt like the tenth time. I sat down on the workout bench and picked up the fifteen-pound weight for my last set of bicep curls. "Let's not get ahead of ourselves."

"Oh, I know, I know. But come on Charlie! He could be your happily ever after. This could be your first date with your future husband!"

I busted out laughing. "I guarantee if you tell Brody that, it'll be my last date with him, too."

We broke into a fit of giggles, and I had a difficult time finishing my last set before Coach Tanner called it.

"Alright, that's time!" he called out. "Good job this morning. I'll see all of you later."

"Good job, girl. We killed it." Allison gave me a high five. "I've got to run, but you have fun on that date of yours."

"I'll tell you all about it later."

"You better!"

When she left the room, I packed my water bottle and towel into my bag and made my way to Brody, who was using one of those foam rollers to stretch his legs. Before I reached him, my cell phone started to ring. I groaned and pulled it out of my bag. It wasn't a number I recognized, but I decided to answer it anyway.

"Is this Charlotte Price?" A man asked when I answered the phone.

"This is she. Can I ask who's calling?"

"This is Ben Davis, I am the owner of Fit Happens Gym. One of our personal trainers, Allison Benson, mentioned you were looking

91

for a management position. I would like to invite you to come in for an interview this afternoon."

"Of course!" I exclaimed, my voice full of surprise. I didn't know he would get back to me this quickly. Allison only talked to him yesterday. "I have practice until three, but I can come in after, say 3:30, if that works for you?"

"Yes, my son, Landon swims with you, so I know about your schedule. That time is fine. Please bring an extra resume with you. Let me give you the address." I put him on speaker and entered the address into my phone.

"Thank you, Mr. Davis, I'll see you at 3:30!"

"I look forward to speaking with you Ms. Price." He ended the call, and I stuck my phone back into my bag. I beamed from ear to ear. I would have to go home after lunch to grab a nice pair of clothes and a copy of my resume.

"Hey, was that good news?" Brody chuckled as he approached. He was wearing only black athletic shorts, and he used a towel to dab away the sweat on his face. "You look like you just won the lottery."

"Yes, it was very good news. I have an interview at the gym where Allison works this afternoon."

He offered me a high five, which I quickly accepted. He clasped his fingers around mine when our hands met, and he held on for a beat longer than I expected him to.

"Congratulations! That's big news. Do we need to postpone lunch?"

"No, I can still go," I said, dropping my hand from his. "It just might have to be a quickie."

"I've become the master of quickies, so that shouldn't be an issue for me." He winked at me.

"Very classy, Brody." I gave him a playful punch on the shoulder. "I'm telling you now that this is literally only going to be lunch. Nothing else is going to happen, so if you have other ideas, we might as well—"

"Oh, lighten up, I'm joking!" He burst out laughing. "You walked into that one yourself, I had to take advantage of it. I'm going to get dressed. I'll meet you out front in ten." When he turned to go to the locker room, I couldn't help but smile at his joke.

It was a *little* funny.

A few minutes later, after a quick shower and a change of clothes, I met Brody outside in front of the building. It was another dreadfully hot day, but also looked like it could rain. The clouds offered us a little relief from the blazing sun.

"You ready?" he asked when he saw me.

"Sure am. Where do you want to go?"

"I've got a place in mind. What if we go to—"

"Hi Brody!" A little girl, who couldn't have been older than eight, came running up to us from somewhere in the parking lot.

"Well, hey there, Miss Lily!" Brody laughed and caught the girl as she came barreling into his arms. "Are you here to swim?"

"I am! Mom said I'm going to be as fast as you someday." She stood back and flexed her little muscles to show him how strong she was getting.

Brody crouched down so he was at her eye level. "I bet you'll be even faster than me if you keep working hard."

"I don't know about that!" She giggled.

"Let me introduce you to my friend here," Brody said, pointing to me. "This is Charlie. She just started swimming with me. She's really fast, too. She might be your competition someday." He winked at me.

She waved to me. "Hi Charlie, my name is Lily."

"It's nice to meet you, Lily. Do you have a favorite stroke?" I asked her.

"Yeah, I like backstroke."

"No way! Me too." I held out my hand for a high five and she smacked it with all her might.

"Lily! You can't go running off without me." Her mother came bounding through the parking lot a moment later, carrying a newborn in her arms. "Oh, Brody. I'm glad she found you. This one likes to run off." She reached her daughter's side and smoothed some of Lily's hair out of her face.

"It's my pleasure, Mrs. Devlin. Seeing Lily is always a joy." He smiled. "Say, there's now going to be a swim clinic here this weekend if Lily would be interested in signing up?"

"Really? I hadn't seen any notifications or bulletins. When did they decide to put that together?"

"This morning actually." Brody chuckled. "But Charlie and I and our other teammates will be working the event. I think Lily would do

93

great." He leaned down to give Lily another high five. "And we'd get to hang out some more. What do you say to that?"

"I want to do it!" She started jumping up and down excitedly. "Can I, mom? Please?

"Well, I don't see why not." Lily's mom smiled. "Where can I sign her up?"

"My Coach can probably help you with that. I can take you to his office really quick if you'd like?" He turned his attention to me. "That's okay, right? It should only take a few minutes."

I nodded. "Yeah, that's totally fine! I'll just wait out here. It was nice meeting you, Lily."

"You, too!" she said excitedly as she followed Brody and her mother into the gym.

I took a seat on one of the benches outside the front door and pulled my phone out to check my messages. I sent a quick text off to Allison to let her know that I got an interview at the gym, and to thank her for the hundredth time for recommending me.

A few minutes passed, and I was starting to feel a bit warm sitting in the heat. I closed my eyes and fanned my face with my hand in an attempt to cool off a little.

"Mind if I join you?" a female voice said, nearly making me jump out of my seat.

I opened my eyes and saw Camila standing before me, a too-sweet smile plastered on her face.

Hadn't she left a few hours ago? What was she still doing here?

"Sorry, I didn't mean to startle you," she said. She sat down beside me even though I hadn't responded to her question. "It's Charlie, right?" she asked.

"Yes," I said curtly. I wasn't really in the mood to talk to her, especially considering how rude she had been to me this morning.

"Look, I wanted to apologize for my rude behavior this morning," she said as though she were reading my mind. "I was in a bad mood, and I took it out on you. I'm sorry. That wasn't fair of me to do."

I nodded. "That's okay," I said, hoping she would drop it.

"Let me make it up to you." She grabbed my hand with both of hers and held onto it as though we were best friends. "I want to take you to lunch. Anywhere you like, my treat. What do you say?"

I tried to hide the surprise that was probably written all over my face. This Camila was a total 180 shift from the Camila I met this morning. "Well, I kind of already have lunch plans today," I told her. "Maybe some other time?"

"Let me guess, you're getting lunch with Brody?" The smile that had been on her face a moment ago, disappeared immediately.

"Actually, yes," I said with caution.

She was practically scowling at me now, and I was getting anxious thinking about how she was going to react. Brody was her ex, after all, and some women got super crazy jealous even after the relationship was over. I tried to scoot further down the bench and pull my hand away from her, but she tightened her grip.

"Can I give you a little advice? Girlfriend to girlfriend?" She was no longer scowling, but she wasn't exactly smiling either.

I nodded nervously. I didn't know what she had to say, but it didn't sound like it was going to be good.

"Be careful around Brody. He may seem all sweet and wonderful now, but give it time. He'll get bored with you, just like he did with me."

"What do you mean by that?" I had a feeling I already knew what she meant, but I asked anyway.

"I mean, he likes to take advantage of the fact that he's a famous professional swimmer," she said. "He knows the effect he has on the ladies."

That sounded an awful lot like what Allison had said the other day.

"When he gets bored," Camila continued. "He seeks out that attention. I'm not sure how many times he did it, but when I caught him in bed with my best friend, I had to call it quits for us. It wasn't fair to me."

I felt my heart plummet to the bottom of my stomach. I was worried Brody was a bit of a lady's man, but Allison had assured me he was capable of being in a committed relationship. Maybe she didn't know Brody as well as she thought she did. Then, another thing Allison told me popped into my head.

"Yesterday, Allison told me that your relationship with Brody ended because *you* did him wrong," I said to Camila, trying like hell to keep my tears at bay. "Why would she say that if it wasn't true?"

Camila's eyes widened for a split second, but she shrugged it off. "I don't know why she would say that, Charlie. Maybe Brody was trying to make me look like the bad guy."

"She did say he didn't tell her any other details."

"That's your answer then, I think."

A few tears escaped despite my efforts, and I had to look away from Camila so she wouldn't see. I tried to dab at them with the back of my free hand without her noticing, but it was no use.

"Hey, there's no need to cry," she said. "My goal wasn't to make you upset. I just wanted to warn you, so you didn't end up in the same situation that I did."

"Well, thanks, I guess," I sniffed. I still didn't look at her. I kind of just wanted to be alone, and I hoped she'd take the hint.

"But if you still choose to have lunch with Brody this afternoon, don't say I didn't warn you," she continued to push the subject.

"Camila," I said, possibly a little too harshly. "You've said what you had to say. I get it. I'm not trying to be rude, but please, can you leave me alone so I can process this?"

She dropped my hand from hers and jumped out of her seat. "Of course, I'm so sorry!" she said, not sounding very sorry at all. "I'll just be on my way, then. Keep that lunch date in mind." She turned and sauntered away as if she didn't have a care in the world.

I wasn't sure which lunch date she was referring to in her parting words, but something told me it wasn't a reference towards the two of us getting lunch someday. She was making one last attempt to convince me not to go with Brody.

Stealing a glance towards the door of the gym, I didn't see any sign of Brody returning. I had no idea how much of what Camila said was true, but I no longer felt like waiting around for him. I was more confused than I was before, and I was starting to wonder if Brody was even worth the trouble.

How could I be happy in a relationship, if I was constantly going to be questioning his intentions? I now had three different perspectives of him—one from Camila, one from Allison, and one from Brody himself—and I had no idea what to believe anymore. But I did know one thing: I wasn't going to sit around and wait to be made a fool of.

Maybe I was wrong to give in and jump into a new relationship already. This was all happening so fast, anyway. I only met him a few days ago. He was distracting me from what I had come to Florida to do in the first place. Maybe this really wasn't worth all the heartache.

Making my decision, I stood from the bench and left without looking back.

Chapter Eleven

Brody

"Here we go! I found them." Coach Tanner was on his computer looking for the signup forms Roman had sent him for the swim clinic this weekend. "Sorry about the wait, I just found out about all of this, this morning. I'll print a few copies off for you."

"No problem at all, I appreciate your help," Mrs. Devlin said.

Coach started to print the copies, and the two of them chatted about the swim clinic while they waited for them to finish. Lily was talking my ear off about learning how to swim all the strokes, and how she wanted to teach her younger brother when he was old enough to learn. I was only half-listening though. I was focused on trying to hurry this along so I could get back out to Charlie.

I honestly couldn't remember the last time I was this excited about spending time with a girl, and sex had nothing to do with it. I wanted to get to know this girl. What was her favorite food, what did she do for fun, did she have any other interests outside of swimming? I wanted to know it all.

Smiling and nodding to whatever Lily had just said, I let my gaze wander to the window in Coach Tanner's office. He had a view of the front parking lot, and I could see the bench where Charlie was waiting for me if I craned my neck enough. However, this time when I looked out at her, she wasn't sitting alone.

Shit.

She was talking to Camila.

Without thinking, I jumped up from my chair and went straight to the window to get a better look. Whatever they were talking about was clearly upsetting Charlie. She was trying to wipe away tears with her hand, and I knew I had to get out there, and fast.

"What are you looking at?" Lily's small voice came from beside me. She was looking out the window too, trying to find whatever had caught my attention.

"I thought I saw a squirrel," I lied.

"I love squirrels!" she squealed.

I thought she would. "Coach, I need to get going," I said. "Do you need anything else from me?"

"Yes, I'd actually love your help hanging up these information sheets about the swim clinic." He handed me a stack of papers. "Could you post these on all the bulletins throughout the building?"

"Can I do it when I come back this afternoon?" I asked, getting impatient. "I *really* need to get going."

"Brody, it'll take five minutes." Coach sounded annoyed. "We need to get the word out quickly since Roman gave us such short notice."

I groaned but agreed to do it. Waving goodbye to Lily and her mom, I beelined it out of Coach Tanner's office. I literally ran through the gym, pinning up the bulletins to all of the boards—there were probably half a dozen or so—and then went straight for the front door.

When I got outside, Camila was no longer there, but neither was Charlie.

"Shit." I combed my fingers through my hair and searched the parking lot for any sign of her, but I didn't see her anywhere. Pulling out my phone, I dialed her number she had given me this morning, but it went straight to voicemail.

Not sure what else to do, I ran to my car and took off for Roman and Camila's house. I was going to get to the bottom of this.

I pulled directly into their driveway this time and sprinted to the door. Instead of ringing the doorbell, I slammed my fists on the door until a very confused maid opened it.

"Can I help you, sir?" she asked, a worried look on her face.

"Is Camila here?" I growled.

"Yes, but she doesn't want to be bothered. Can I give her a message?"

"I'll give it to her myself." I gently pushed the woman aside and marched past her into the house.

"Sir, please!" She came after me, trying to hold me back. "I can't let you just walk in here!"

Ignoring her, I went for the room I almost walked into my first day here. Something told me she would be in there. I reached the door and turned the knob, but it was locked.

I smashed both of my fists onto the door. "Camila!" I shouted. "I know you're in there. We need to talk."

A moment later the door opened a crack and Camila stuck her nose out. "Oh, it's you." She slid through the opening in the door and closed it behind her.

"I'm so sorry, Miss Camila, I tried to stop him," the maid said. "I can have him escorted out."

"That won't be necessary just yet." Camila held up a finger. "What are you doing here, Brody? You've got a lot of nerve barging into my house like this."

"What the hell did you say to Charlie?" I barked.

"What do you mean?" she said. "We just had a lovely chat about getting lunch together sometime."

"Then why did she leave? We were supposed to have lunch today."

"Oh, were you? Hmm, I had no idea." She placed a hand on her chin and feigned concern.

Grabbing her by the shoulders, I pressed her hard against the wall. "Cut the crap, what did you say to her?"

"Careful, Brody." She smirked. "I'd hate to tell Roman you were harassing me on top of everything else you've done."

"Tell me what you said!" I shouted. I was getting more pissed off the longer I stood there.

Just then, a loud clunk and some cussing came from the other side of Camila's door. The smirk on her face faded immediately, as well as all the color in her face.

"What was that?" I asked. "Is someone else in there?"

"It's none of your concern," she spat.

"Are you cheating on Roman?"

"Of course not, I would never—"

"I think we both know you would." I cut her off. "You have before, remember?"

She narrowed her eyes and remained speechless for a long moment.

"Get out," she said finally. "GET OUT!"

"Camila—"

"Get out of my house, Brody! I will call the cops!"

I released her shoulders from my grip and took a few steps back. "This isn't over," I said. "I'm going to find out what you told Charlie, *and* what's going on in there."

Camila scowled at me, but I didn't wait around to see if she had anything else to say. Something strange was definitely going on, and I was going to find out what it was, but right now, I had to make things right with Charlie.

******

When I returned to the pool for my afternoon swim, I was still fuming from what had happened with Camila. I had no idea what she said to Charlie, and I was worried that whatever she said caused some damage. I tried calling and texting her, but she didn't respond. She was pissed, and I needed to find out why.

I was early for swim practice, and paced the pool deck while I waited for Charlie to show. She was usually early too, so I hoped that was the case today as well. I needed time to talk to her before we had to get started.

After what felt like an eternity later, Charlie finally walked out of the locker room with her head down and went to the first bench to set down her things. She turned her back to me and stayed that way while she dug through her bag for her cap and goggles.

Not wanting to wait any longer, I marched right to her side. "Charlie, what happened?"

She didn't respond or turn around. In fact, she didn't react at all. Almost as if she didn't hear me.

"Charlie," I said as gently as I could, even though all of my nerve endings felt like they were on fire. I reached for her shoulder and turned her to face me.

Her eyes were red and a little puffy from crying. "Brody, please, I don't want to get into this," she mumbled. "I'm tired of being confused. This is too much for me. I need to focus on what I came here to do."

"Please tell me what Camila told you. I could see you from Coach Tanner's office window. I tried to get out there sooner, but you were already gone. What did she say to you?"

"It doesn't matter. I don't know who to trust, and I'm tired of this emotional roller coaster." She tried to shove past me, but I reached for her hand and stopped her.

"You can trust me, Charlie."

"Can I, though?" she asked, clearly getting upset again. "Everyone keeps telling me you're a lady's man. That you take advantage of being famous to get laid. You even tried to get me in bed with you the first day we met. Is this all a game to you? I'm starting to think you'll say anything you can to get in my pants, and then I'll be gone like the rest of them. You'll get bored of me."

"Get bored of you?" I asked, confused. "Charlie, I'll admit that I haven't wanted a relationship for a while, especially how things ended with Camila—"

"That's another thing!" She nearly yelled, throwing her arms in the air. "She told me you cheated on her with her best friend. Who the hell does that? If we were to start dating, how long would it take for you to go fuck my best friend?"

"What the hell? Is that what she told you?" I clenched my fists, trying my hardest to hold back the anger that was boiling inside me. "Charlie, I never cheated on Camila. *She* cheated on *me*."

"What?"

"Yeah, that's why I finally pulled the plug on the relationship. I came home one night, and she was in my house screwing my former manager." I was seeing red just remembering that night. It wasn't something I talked about. I never told anyone—except Chase—before now exactly what had happened.

"Are you serious?" Charlie asked, her mouth hanging open.

"Dead serious. I was thinking about ending the relationship anyway, since she had more interest in my paycheck than me, but that night put the final nail in the coffin. I fired my manager that day too, had to hire someone else." I talked calmly despite the emotions I was feeling reliving that night.

"Brody, I'm sorry," she said, her voice dropped several octaves. "Camila told me you got bored with her."

"And you believed her?" I asked. "Charlie, I haven't lied to you once since I've met you. I may have said some stupid stuff, but it's what I felt at the time. You can trust that I will be honest with you."

She remained speechless, but I could see the realization wash over her face as she thought about it.

"Have I been with a lot of girls in the past? Maybe not a *lot*, but a few, sure," I continued. "Did I want a relationship with you at first? I'll admit I didn't. I was seeing a beautiful girl that was checking me out, and I assumed you wanted what I wanted. I'm a guy, what can I say? Sometimes we are pigs."

She pinched her lips together to hide her smile.

I took her hand in mine again. "Charlie, I told you before: I can't explain these feelings I'm having. I don't know why I feel like I'm being drawn to you, but I want to explore this. I—"

"I need to have a word with you two!" Coach Tanner's voice boomed behind us, startling us both. We jumped apart, her hand dropping from mine.

"We'll talk later," I whispered to Charlie before Coach Tanner approached.

She gave me a simple nod.

"Have a seat," Coach Tanner demanded.

Charlie and I exchanged a quick glance and did as we were told.

"I just received a phone call from Roman." Coach Tanner crossed his arms and frowned down at us. "I have to say I am incredibly disappointed in what he told me."

Charlie shot me another nervous glance before she answered. "What did he say? Did something fall through with the swim clinic?"

"No, it had nothing to do with the clinic. It was about the two of you."

Shit. I had a feeling I knew what this was about.

"I heard from Roman that the two of you were harassing Camila this morning."

"What?" Both Charlie and I said at the same time.

"What exactly is she claiming?" I asked. From what Charlie told me, it sounded like Camila had been the one harassing her, not the other way around.

"Roman said Camila had asked Charlie to have lunch with her sometime, and Charlie called her a bitch and made her upset."

Charlie's mouth dropped open. "Coach Tanner, I swear that's not what happened. Camila did ask me to go to lunch, but I told her—"

Coach Tanner held up a hand. "Charlie, I believe you. I thought it was rather childish of Camila to say such a thing, especially when I know you are not that kind of person. I simply wanted you to confirm that my suspicion was correct." His gaze then turned towards me. "However, Roman also happened to mention that Brody here showed up uninvited to their house and was harassing and frightening Camila."

"You did?" Charlie whipped around to face me, a look of surprise and confusion on her face.

"I wish I could say that sounded like a lie as well, Brody, but given your track record, I have a feeling this one might be true."

I didn't say anything. Instead, I lowered my gaze, trying to avoid both of their stares.

Coach Tanner threw his arms up in exasperation. "Brody, why do you keep getting yourself into these kinds of situations? You're lucky that woman hasn't filed a restraining order against you, and *really* lucky that Roman hasn't pulled any funding for this team. This can't keep happening."

"Wait, this has happened before?" Charlie asked in disbelief.

"Last week, he went and bashed the poor man's car in because he thought it was Camila's!" Coach Tanner started pacing back and forth in front of us. "For the love of God, Brody, you need to get over this woman!"

"Hold on, I told you that wasn't me!" I blurted. I faced Charlie, my eyes pleading with her. "You have to believe me. I didn't smash her car, and I don't have feelings for her anymore." I lowered my voice so only Charlie could hear, "I only want you."

Her eyes searched mine for several seconds, as if she were searching for the truth. After a moment, she looked away.

"Charlie—"

"That's enough, Brody," Coach Tanner finally said. He stopped pacing in front of us with his hands on his hips. "It stops now. I can't keep getting you out of trouble. Do you hear me?"

"Yes sir," I said. I stole another glance at Charlie. "It won't happen again."

"Good. Even so, Roman insists on punishing the two of you for your actions."

Charlie sat up a little straighter and her brow furrowed in confusion.

"Why is Charlie being punished?" I beat her to the question. "You even said yourself that you believed she didn't do anything."

"I know, but Roman believes Camila is telling him the truth," Coach Tanner sighed.

"What's the punishment?" Charlie asked.

"Both of you will be going over to Howard Enterprises after the swim clinic on Saturday, and he has a number of cleaning chores lined up for the two of you."

"So, now I'm going to be cleaning his house *and* his office?" I couldn't hide the anger from my voice.

Charlie shot me a glance, and I immediately regretted saying anything in front of her. I forgot she didn't know I was "working" for Roman and Camila. If she's still talking to me after this, she's going to have a lot of questions.

"No, you won't be working at their house anymore," Coach said. "Camila insists that she doesn't want you anywhere near there. He said you are done working for him, but you will write a check for the remainder of the vehicle damages. The check will go directly to Camila."

Of course, it would. Looked like Camila was getting her way again. We would be out of her way, *and* she got all the money for the car damage. Damage made to a car that wasn't even *hers*.

"So, what if we refuse to do it?" I asked.

"Roman said if you don't show up, he will pull funding for our next swim meet. So, if you want to compete, you'll go."

I opened my mouth to argue, but Coach Tanner stopped me. "I don't want to hear any more from you, Brody. If you're going to act like a child, you'll be treated like one." He turned around and went over to his marker board to write the workout. "We are late starting practice. Let's get in and get started."

Charlie stood up to go, but I grabbed her hand to stop her. "Charlie, please let me explain."

"We have practice." She didn't look at me and jerked her hand from my grasp.

I ran my hands through my hair as I watched her walk away. This hole I was in just kept getting deeper. If I didn't change something soon, I wasn't sure how I was going to get myself out of it.

Chapter Twelve

Charlie

As soon as practice was over, I snatched up my equipment and darted off to the locker room to get ready for my interview. I was excited for the interview itself, and I was also thankful for the excuse to get going and avoid being around Brody afterwards. He may have denied having feelings for Camila, but why did he keep acting out towards her? Something strange was going on, and I really didn't feel like talking about it right now. This emotional roller coaster ride didn't appear to be coming to an end any time soon.

Limited on time, I ran through the shower and got ready as quickly as I could. I threw my hair into a twist on the top of my head, put a touch of makeup on, and got dressed in my interview attire. Wearing a pair of slim-fitting black dress pants with a matching blazer and a white blouse underneath, I felt ready to take on the business world. I slipped into my favorite pair of black pumps and was on my way out.

Pulling into the parking lot of Fit Happens Gym just in time, I took a deep breath and went inside. Once in the building, I was delighted to see how nice the place was. There were several options of free weights and various weight machines on one end of the gym, and several different cardio machines on the other end. It wasn't too busy at this hour, with maybe only a dozen people or so working out.

After another quick scan around the building, I located Allison by the free weights with a client. She looked up from what she was doing and waved to me. When I waved back, she gave me a thumbs up and mouthed the words 'Good luck!' I couldn't help but smile. I was still smiling as I walked up to the main counter where a young man in his early twenties stood at the computer.

"Hi, I'm Charlie Price," I said to him as I approached. "I have a 3:30 interview with Mr. Davis."

"Sure, I'll get him for you." The young man returned my smile before he turned and disappeared into an office to the left of the counter.

"Charlotte Price?" a large man called as he followed the front desk boy out of the office.

"That's me." I held my hand out to shake his. "But please, call me Charlie. It's nice to meet you, Mr. Davis."

"Likewise, Charlie. Come with me." He waved his muscular arm, directing me to follow him. He was very tall, probably 6'5", and his muscles were so large they nearly popped out of his blue polo. He was big-boned, and everything about him was just huge. He looked like he was in his upper forties, with dark, straight hair cut close to his head.

"Please, have a seat." He motioned to an empty chair once we had entered his office. It was surprisingly smaller than I expected, and with no windows, it felt rather cramped.

"Thanks for meeting with me, Mr. Davis," I said as I handed him my resume.

"No problem at all. Allison had nothing but good things to say about you, and we have been looking to hire a new manager for a while now," he said as he glanced through my recent experiences. "Shall we get started?"

He asked me questions about my experience, why I would be the best fit for his gym, and what ideas I could bring to improve his business, and all of the questions one would normally ask during an interview.

The longer the interview went on, the harder it was for me to understand why Allison didn't get along with him. He was pleasant to talk to, polite, and overall seemed to be a pretty cool guy.

"I'll tell you what," Mr. Davis said after I finished telling him my ideas for the place. "I am going to make this quick for both of us. I want to offer you the job. I think having two professional swimmers employed here will really help with business." He began gathering papers and shuffling items around on his desk without looking up at me. "Now, if I could just find a pen, we can get the paperwork started."

Unease crept into my stomach at his comment. "Sir, if you don't mind me saying: I really hope I am being hired based on my merit and my experience, and not because of my swimming career."

He waved his hands in front of him. "No, of course not. I am impressed with your background, and I really like your vision for the place. The fact that you're a professional swimmer is just an added bonus. Are you interested in accepting?"

I nodded. "I'm interested. Allison said she really likes working here, so I think it would be a great place to work. What is the pay, if you don't mind me asking?"

He folded his hands on top of his desk. "The best I can do is eighteen dollars an hour, and I expect you to work up to twenty hours a week. I've recently had to drop healthcare benefits, so I hope that won't be an issue."

Normally, yes, that would be an issue. But I got all my health coverage through American Swimming, so it didn't make a huge difference to me. "That's totally fine," I told him.

"So, do we have a deal?" He reached his hand across his desk, inviting me to shake it.

Hesitating for only a split second, I shook his hand and smiled. "Yes, I'd love to accept the job. Thank you, Mr. Davis."

"Great!" He slid the paperwork across the desk towards me. "We'll just get to work on filling this out, and then I can give you a quick tour of the place."

******

An hour later, after Mr. Davis had given me the full tour and I finished filling out all the paperwork, I was officially the evening manager of Fit Happens Gym. I was so thrilled I was able to find a job this quickly, and it felt as if a giant weight had been lifted off my shoulders as my new life in Jacksonville fell into place.

However, there was still one issue that continued to linger in my mind, and it had everything to do with Brody. He hadn't left my thoughts once as I tried to piece together everything I learned today. Whether he was truly over Camila or not, there was no denying something was going on between them. Did I really want to get in the middle of it?

Maybe I needed to talk to Allison again. She provided some good insight last time, maybe she would know what this was all about. She told me to come find her after my interview anyway.

I took a glance around the gym and saw her stretching on a yoga mat on the far side of the room. She didn't appear to have any clients with her, so I made my way over.

"There you are!" She jumped up off the ground when she saw me approaching. "I was starting to think you had left without telling me about the interview. How did it go?"

"Sorry about that. I wasn't planning on being here this long, buuuuut," I paused for dramatic effect. "I got the job!"

"Oh, my goodness, congratulations!" Her face lit up, and she pulled me in for a hug. "I knew you would, I had no doubt in my mind."

"I owe it all to you. Thank you so much for talking to him for me. Your raving review must have won him over."

"Well, that probably helped, but let's be real, you sealed the deal, honey. I can't take the credit for that."

"Fine, but I owe you. Seriously, just say the word."

"You can buy the wine and pizza tomorrow night," she chuckled, referring to the Friday night plans we had made after lunch yesterday. "And I get to pick what movie we watch!"

"It's hard to say no to that." I laughed with her. "But seriously, I can't thank you enough. You really helped me out this week."

"Girl, it was no trouble at all. I'm just glad you got it, and now I have a friend at both jobs!"

"That you do." I smiled. "So, how long until you get off?"

"Technically, I'm done now. My last client didn't show up this evening, so I was just doing some stretches. Otherwise, I'd typically be here until 5:30 on Tuesdays and Thursdays."

"So, do you have a few minutes to chat?" I asked hopefully.

"Of course, what's going on?"

I told her all about the events of the morning, how Brody and I had planned to go to lunch, but Camila came and ruined everything. I told her about the phone call from Roman, and how Brody and I were now expected to work for him this weekend. I found myself growing frustrated once more replaying everything aloud.

"Do you know if Brody still has feelings for her?" I asked Allison when I had finished explaining.

"I don't think so." She shook her head. "He tries to avoid her as much as he physically can, and if he told you he doesn't have feelings for her, then I believe him. However, I don't have a good explanation for his actions. He can be a hot-head sometimes, but smashing a car? Showing up at someone's house and threatening them? That seems strange—even for Brody."

"I thought so, too," I sighed. "I'm trying to decide if it's even worth getting into anything with him right now. I can't keep second-guessing everything—"

"Then talk to him!" She pressed, grasping both of my shoulders. "He hasn't lied to you so far. What makes you think he'd start now?"

I shrugged. "I don't know."

"Then you need to talk to him. Get the answers right from the source. I'm willing to help in any way I can, Charlie, but I don't know what's going on between Brody and Camila any more than you do."

"You're right, I'm sorry," I pouted. "This has just been such a challenge in such a short amount of time."

"No one said relationships were easy," she chuckled. She dropped her hands from my shoulders and pulled me into another hug. "They take work. It's not easy to get Brody to open up, I can tell you that much. If he's making an effort to talk to you about these kinds of things, then he's seriously trying to make something work with you. I think you need to show him the same kind of effort on your end if you want anything to come of this."

Hugging her tighter, I sighed into her shoulder. "You're right … again."

She broke the hug after a few moments and held me at arm's length once more. "One thing you'll soon find out is that I usually am." She winked.

I couldn't help but laugh. "I'm already figuring that out. I'll talk to Brody."

"Promise?" she asked.

"Promise."

******

I couldn't gather the courage to talk to Brody on Friday, and Allison gave me a ton of crap for it during our pizza and movie night. She told me if I didn't say anything to Brody at the swim clinic, then I would have to pay for the wine and pizza every week for a month, so I showed up extra early on Saturday morning in hopes I'd have time to talk to him.

110

When I got to the pool, I saw Allison sitting on the bleachers, sorting out a pile of papers that were resting in her lap. Although the swim clinic didn't begin for at least another 30 minutes, there were already a handful of kids sitting in the bleachers with their parents waiting for us to begin. Half of the adults had their noses buried in their cell phones, while the other half were trying to get their children to stop running through the stands.

I sent a silent *thank you* to Coach Tanner for canceling our early swim practice today. I needed the extra rest if I was going to deal with all this energy. I waved at some of the kids as I made my way towards Allison.

"Hey, have you seen Brody yet?" I took a seat beside her. I set my swim bag down next to hers and she passed me a handful of the papers she was sorting.

"Not yet. Can you help me sort these? They are the rosters for each of us. We will each have about twelve kids."

"Sure." I took the pile she handed me and started shuffling.

By the time we finished sorting and reviewing drills, Brody came strolling inside. Allison and I said good morning to him, but he simply smiled and nodded and continued to walk past us. He stopped a few feet away and set his things down on one of the benches.

"Now's your chance," Allison whispered to me. "You don't have a lot of time, but it's enough to clear the air."

"No pressure or anything." I took a deep breath. She whispered good luck and gave me a slight nudge in Brody's direction. I slowly stood and made my way over to him, mentally preparing what I was going to say to him.

"Guys, can you come into my office please?" Coach Tanner stuck his head out the door of his office and motioned for us to come quickly. I stole a glance back at Allison who just pouted and shrugged her shoulders. I'd have to try and catch Brody later.

"Where's Landon?" Coach asked once we were packed inside his small office.

"Haven't seen him yet." Brody shrugged.

"Can you send him a message and make sure he didn't forget? He's cutting it kind of close." Coach Tanner shook his head. "Sorry if I seem a little frazzled this morning. Roman stopped answering

111

his phone, and left me hanging on some of the last-minute details. I've been trying to get everything pulled together myself."

"Shocker," Brody mumbled.

"Watch it, Brody." Coach narrowed his eyes at him. "So, is everything ready to go out there? Allison, you were able to get the papers organized?"

"Yep, Charlie and I divided up the roster sheets and the lane lines are already in, so we should be set to go with everything," Allison said, handing Brody and me our sheets.

"Great, thank you. Let's head out there then." Coach went to rise from his chair, but before he did so, Landon came rushing into the office.

"I'm here," he said out of breath. "Sorry, I know I'm late."

"Landon, I told you to be here at least twenty minutes early." Coach leaned back in his chair and threw his hands up in front of him, clearly upset.

"I know, I'm sorry. My dad was busy and couldn't drive me this morning. I had to take the bus, but I missed the early one and had to wait," he started rambling.

"It's okay, Landon," Coach stopped him. "You're here now, that's what matters. Next time, please don't hesitate to give me a call. I'd be more than happy to give you a ride. Now, let's get out there and get started, okay?"

We filed out of the office and back onto the pool deck, where the stands had filled up with a bunch of excited kids waiting to begin.

"Landon, why didn't you just stay at my house?" I heard Brody say to Landon from behind me.

"I can't stay there *every* night," Landon shot back. "I was fine until I needed to leave this morning." He started walking faster to catch up with Coach Tanner, and left Brody behind. I lingered for a moment so Brody could catch up to me.

"Did you hear that?" he asked, the curiosity on my face giving me away. He shook his head. "It's better if you don't ask any questions. He'd just be embarrassed if more people knew."

I pressed my lips together and fought the urge to argue with him. Now wasn't the time or the place to make a scene.

"Good morning everyone!" Coach Tanner called out to the crowd. He held up his palms to quiet everyone down. "Thanks for coming out this morning. My swimmers and I are very excited to welcome all of you, and we are ready to have some fun!"

The kids erupted into little cheers, and I noticed a few of them were yelling out Brody's name, begging to be put into his group. It was only natural they would want to be with the most famous one, I guess.

"Now, I'm going to assign each of you to one of my swimmers here," Coach Tanner continued. "We will do one group at a time, please stay seated until I have finished calling off all the names in the group, then you can *walk* down here and join your coach for the day. We'll start with Brody's group first."

Brody stepped forward and waved to everyone as Coach started calling off names for his group. When all the names were called, Coach had to yell at quite a few kids who were trying to run down and be the first to talk to Brody. When they reached him, all of them were trying to hug him at the same time, and he hugged each of them in turn. I had to admit, it was kind of cute.

Coach went on with calling kids down and a few minutes later, we each had our own group of kids and proceeded to our designated sections of the pool. Luckily, I did part-time coaching gigs and taught swimming lessons all through college, so I wasn't too nervous about working with the kids today. At least, I wasn't nervous until my kids started complaining that they had to be in my group when they wanted to be with Brody.

"Why do we have to be in *your* group?" A small blonde girl who couldn't have been older than nine whined at me. "We wanted to meet Brody Hayes!"

I shouldn't have been surprised. I was too new, no one knew who I was, but the little girl's comment still stung a little.

"Be quiet, Emily. This is Brody's friend. She's nice," said another little girl. I noticed it was Lily, the girl I had met the other day when I was with Brody.

"Thank you, Lily. It's good to see you again." I smiled at her. "Maybe you guys can meet Brody before the end of the day, but for now you're stuck with me. How about we get in the water and do a nice and easy 200 freestyle to get loosened up?"

One by one, the kids jumped into our two designated lanes. While they warmed up, I ditched my t-shirt and shorts on a bench and stole a glance over in Brody's direction. Allison was talking to him while the kids were warming up, and I wondered if she was saying anything about me. The odds were probably slim, but I couldn't help but wonder regardless.

For the next few hours I tried to concentrate on the swimming drills, instead of Brody. It was easier said than done, though. Every time a kid complained about not being in his group, I would start thinking about him all over again.

Throughout the morning, I found myself stealing more glances over at him to watch him work with the kids. He handled it with such ease and seemed to be enjoying himself. I couldn't help the smile that spread across my face as I watched. There was nothing sexier than a man who was good with kids, and I could feel my heart flutter every time I looked over at him.

"Look, Mom! Even our coach would rather be in Brody's group!" The same little blonde girl from earlier yelled out loud enough for the whole pool to hear. A brief moment of silence fell over the entire room as everyone turned to look at me at the same time. I felt my face turn a million different shades of red as I turned towards the child's mother to give her an apologetic wave. Luckily—for me—the woman looked just as embarrassed as I was.

I turned to face Brody to gauge his reaction, and he was looking right at me. He was smiling, and it was hard to tell from here, but I'm certain he was blushing as well.

A moment later he redirected his attention back to his kids. "Alright guys, let's get back to that breaststroke drill now!"

I finished off the last of the drills with no more embarrassment, and then the kids were to put their new skills to the test with a short workout.

"Can we join Brody's group *now*?" One of the little boys whined when I finished explaining the workout to them.

"You know what? Sure, why not? Let's go over there." I mostly agreed because I was sick and tired of the kids whining about being forced into my group all day. But I also agreed because this seemed like a good opportunity to talk to Brody. The kids would be doing their workout, and I would be free to sneak a few words in with him. All my kids quickly hopped out of the pool and hustled down to the lanes where Brody's kids were at.

"Hey guys, what are you doing?" Brody chuckled when my kids started jumping into his lanes.

"They wouldn't stop complaining about not being in your group. I finally gave in. Hope that's okay," I explained to him as I walked up to him.

"Are you that bad of a coach?" He winked at me and playfully nudged me with his elbow. "It's fine, we were just about to start the set, too." He explained the set one more time for the kids, and we sent them off.

I debated with myself how long to wait before saying anything to Brody. I didn't want to ambush him right away, but also didn't want to waste any time. There were too many questions I wanted answers for. Finally, I decided to just suck it up and go for it.

"Brody, I need to talk to you—"

He held up his hand to stop me. "Let me say something first." He stole one more glance at the kids before turning his attention back to me. "I'm sorry about the other day. I didn't have a chance to explain myself. I'll admit I did go to Camila's house to confront her. I was trying to figure out what she said to you, and I didn't know what else to do. But I did *not* smash her car. That was my buddy, Chase. Long story, I'll tell you later. Anyway, I'm not saying what I did was right, and I wish I had a better reason for doing it, but I can promise you I don't have feelings for Camila. I haven't for a long time."

His eyes were full of sincerity, and I was pretty sure he was telling me the truth, but I was still wary.

"What will happen if you get bored of me?" I asked quietly. "You'll tell me, right? You won't lead me on?"

"Of course, I'll tell you." He nodded. "But I don't see myself getting bored of you anytime soon."

"I need honesty and open communication from you, Brody. This isn't going to work if you can't give me that."

"I know, and I plan to be completely transparent with you from here on out," he said tenderly. "Please give me a chance. If you have any doubts whatsoever, come to me. We'll talk it through. I know I'm not good at this kind of stuff, but I'm willing to try if you are."

I turned my head in an attempt to hide my huge, geeky grin.

Brody placed the tip of his finger on my chin to redirect my attention back to him. "Can I take that as a yes?" He smiled.

I nodded. "Yeah, I'll give this a chance."

115

We held each other's gaze, neither of us saying anything more. We were lost in our own little world until Coach Tanner's voice boomed above all the noise from the kids.

"Alright, that concludes today's clinic! Let's give our coaches a hand for being such wonderful teachers today!" He started clapping his hands and all the kids and parents in the room joined in.

Brody was still staring at me, but I finally broke his gaze and started clapping with everyone else.

"Thanks again for being here everyone," Coach Tanner continued when the noise level dropped. "Kids, please walk back to the locker room or your parents; and parents, please keep an eye out for future clinics we may be holding here. We hope to see you all again soon."

Everyone in the water started getting out and made their way towards the bleachers or the locker rooms. All the kids who were so interested in meeting Brody earlier, now only seemed to be concerned with going home, and they filtered past us quickly with nothing more than a wave goodbye. I waved to some of the kids and went to grab my towel, but before I could move, Brody took hold of my elbow, and pulled me away from the crowd of kids. I resisted slightly at first, unsure what he was doing.

"Come with me," he said.

I made sure Coach, Allison, and Landon were preoccupied before I let Brody lead me away. He quickly pulled me around the corner so that we were out of sight from everyone else. Before I could say anything, he pinned me up against the wall. He pressed his body tight against mine so that I could feel every inch of him.

He placed one of his hands on the back of my neck and gently massaged my cheek with his thumb. "You are so damn beautiful," he whispered.

My stomach fluttered with excitement, and my knees suddenly felt weak. How could he make me feel this way after only a few words?

His gaze lingered on my lips for only a moment before his mouth came crashing down on mine. His one hand still caressed my cheek while his other circled my waist, pulling me even closer to him. I raked my fingers over the tight muscles of his back as he deepened the kiss. There was nothing gentle about the way he ravaged my mouth, and I opened to allow his tongue to swirl against mine. A moan escaped from my throat, and he let out a low grunt in response.

He broke the kiss too soon and pressed his forehead against mine. "I've been wanting to do that since I first laid eyes on you," he whispered. He smiled and closed his eyes as if trying to save this moment to his memory.

I returned his smile and placed a palm on his cheek, pulling him in for one more kiss. "We should probably get back out there before someone realizes we're gone."

Groaning, he took a step away from me so that our bodies were no longer touching. "You're probably right."

"And we have to get ready to go over to Howard Enterprises."

"Don't remind me." He rolled his eyes. "Can we continue this later?"

"We'll see." I winked.

He grabbed my face in both of his hands and kissed me. "Let's make that a yes," he said with a devilish grin.

I giggled and turned to head back to the others on the pool deck. As I walked away, I pressed my fingers to my lips, missing his touch. I couldn't deny the sparks of electricity that were shooting through my body the entire time his hands were on me. I needed more. More of his touch. More of his lips on mine.

We would definitely be continuing this later.

Chapter Thirteen

Brody

While I waited for Roman in the lobby of Howard Enterprises, I replayed the kiss I shared with Charlie over and over in my mind. It was everything I hoped it would be—and more. The spark I felt with her was like nothing I had ever felt before. I'd kissed my fair share of women in the past, but they all paled in comparison.

Was I crazy for having such strong feelings for a woman I'd only known for a week? Was this what love felt like? I thought I loved Camila when I was with her, but even that didn't shine a light in comparison to how I felt when I kissed Charlie. I honestly had no idea what to think about these feelings, but I liked how it felt, and I wanted to keep it going.

I sat up a little straighter when I saw Charlie come through the double doors and enter the lobby. Her presence alone made me light up with excitement. She made her way across the nearly empty room and plopped down beside me on the black leather couch I was sitting on.

"Hey," she said, smiling.

Her smile made me grin like an idiot, and I couldn't hide it if I tried. "Hey, to you too."

"I've been thinking about you."

"Yeah?" I raised my brows expectantly.

"Mhmm." She nodded. "I kind of want you to kiss me again."

"I *really* want to kiss you again," I growled, scooting closer to her.

She leaned in close enough that her lips were nearly on mine. She was so close I could feel her breath on my face as she whispered, "Maybe I'd even let you come over tonight. Pick up where we left off."

God, this girl was going to kill me. This day needed to end soon so I could get my hands on her again.

"I hope I'm not interrupting anything." Camila appeared in front of us, crossing her arms and looking rather annoyed.

Charlie immediately sat back in her seat, jerking herself further away from me. I groaned at Camila's timing. She kept finding ways to swoop in and kill the mood.

"Roman will see you now." She pursed her lips before she swiveled on her heel to return the way she had come.

She herded us into an elevator where we went all the way up to the fifteenth floor. The ride up dragged on painfully slow with all the tension squeezed into one tiny space. Camila stood behind me and I could practically feel her stare burning a hole in the back of my head. Charlie kept fidgeting beside me, stealing glances behind her as if she was worried Camila would attack.

Finally, we reached the top floor and we exited the elevator into Roman's private suite. It took up the entire floor and looked more like a living space than an office. There were several couches and easy chairs scattered about, with at least half a dozen plasma screen TVs anchored to the walls, and on the far end of the floor was Roman's workspace. His desk was well over six feet long, with three computer monitors, and stacks upon stacks of papers and manuals littered across the top.

"Roman, dear, the swimmers are here," Camila said coldly. She walked up to his desk and took a seat on the edge of it.

"Camila, there are plenty of chairs in this office. Please do not sit on my desk," Roman said without looking up from his work. He jotted a few notes down on a pad of paper, and finally stood up with a sigh. He went to Camila's side, kissed her on the cheek, and motioned for her to sit in the chair closest to his desk. When she still didn't move, he wrapped his fingers around her bicep and gently pulled her off of his desk. "Stand if you prefer, sweetheart."

Ignoring her pout, he approached Charlie and me next. "I'm very disappointed that I have to bring the two of you in here today. Especially after what happened with my car, Brody. I was hoping you would have learned your lesson that time. Speaking of which, you brought the check, I presume?"

I took the folded piece of paper out of my pocket and handed it to him. "Made out to Camila, just as you asked." I resisted rolling my eyes. It pissed me off that I was paying for something I didn't even do. But I hadn't spoken to Chase since the night I showed up at his house, and I'd rather just pay off the damages myself instead of bringing it up with him again.

"Very good." He took the check and handed it to Camila. "Anyway, since the two of you have been unbelievably rude to Camila lately, I thought it was only fair to teach you a lesson to

119

ensure it will not happen again, and I'm hoping this lesson will actually stick with you this time, Brody." He shot me a look before he continued. "The bathrooms in my building need cleaning, and I'd like the two of you to tackle that today."

"Don't you have cleaning staff for that?" I asked.

"I normally would, but I have not had the cleaning staff back in my building since the breach. I still haven't figured out who is responsible, and I want to limit how many people have access to my building in the meantime."

"So, just the bathrooms?" Charlie asked.

"Yes, but don't fret," Roman chuckled. "There are four bathrooms per floor—two female, two male—and there are fourteen other floors in this building."

"Holy shit, Roman, we'll be here all night," I told him.

"You will if you don't get moving." He crossed his arms. "There is a small café on the main floor, where you can get something for dinner, but otherwise I expect you to keep working until the job is done. And if you half-ass it, you'll be coming back to do it all again. I want this lesson to actually teach you something. Your swim schedule interfered with your ability to really get anything done when you were working in my home—but not this time. This time, neither of you leaves until the work is done. Do you understand?"

Charlie and I nodded.

"Great. Since it's Saturday, there shouldn't be many people to get in your way. Other than perhaps where my next meeting is taking place." Roman turned his attention back to Camila. "Dear, where exactly would that be?"

"Third floor," she said, handing him a pad of paper.

"Very good. The third floor may need to wait until the end. All the cleaning supplies have already been set up near the restroom on this floor. I suggest you start there and work your way down." He started making his way towards the elevators and motioned for Camila to follow. "I am very busy this afternoon, so please only get a hold of me if there is an emergency. Just ask someone to call Camila, and we will figure out what needs to be done from there." A moment later, the elevator came and Roman and Camila disappeared inside, leaving Charlie and me alone.

"Well, this is pretty shitty," I said after a beat.

"Literally." She gave me a sideways glance and smiled.

I shook my head and let out a low chuckle. "Come on, let's get this over with so we can get out of here."

We started with Roman's personal restroom first as he suggested. We divided up the men's and women's restrooms so that we could cover twice as much ground in the same amount of time. Unfortunately, this meant it wasn't very easy to talk to Charlie while we worked. Time felt like it was passing even slower than usual, and although I tried to clean as quickly as possible, these restrooms were surprisingly filthy for only going a few days without cleaning.

I had no desire to leave Coach Tanner's team, so I'd suck it up and do the cleaning. But there was no way I was going to come back and do this a second time, so I made damn sure everything was spotless before moving on to the next restroom.

After a few hours of work, we were roughly halfway done when Charlie announced she was hungry. She went down to the café and brought back two ham and cheese sandwiches for our dinner break.

"Thank you, I'm starving," I said when she handed me one of the sandwiches. We sat down on the floor next to each other and leaned against the wall to eat.

"I thought you might be. I saw you scrubbing one of those urinals earlier. You were working up a sweat." She laughed and nudged me in the side with her elbow.

I made a face when I remembered which urinal she was referring to. "These people are disgusting."

"Lady's rooms aren't much better," she said. She paused to take a bite of her sandwich. "How late do you think we're going to be here?"

I shrugged and swallowed a bite of my sandwich. "Few more hours at least. Why? You got somewhere to be?"

"I might," she teased. "Supposed to have a hot date tonight."

"A hot date, huh?" I wrapped up my sandwich and put it down beside me. Suddenly, I had an appetite for something else entirely. "What were you going to do on this date?"

She looked at me in between bites, and I could tell she saw the look in my eye that said I wasn't messing around anymore. I couldn't wait until we finished cleaning. I had to kiss her again. Now.

"Well, I suppose we would have dinner first," she suggested.

Reaching for her sandwich, I set it down next to mine. "It appears we have finished that part of the evening, wouldn't you say?"

She nodded, her eyes never leaving mine.

"So, what would come next, Charlie?" I asked, lowering my voice.

"We'd probably sit down on the couch and snuggle in nice and close."

I looked around the floor we were on, but there were no couches in sight. Only small cubicles with swivel chairs, desks, and computers. A sign near the elevator read *IT Department.* "No couches here, but that doesn't mean we can't get a little more comfortable," I said. Grabbing her hand, I pulled her closer to me.

She hesitated for a moment, and then threw one leg over my lap so that she was straddling me. "Is this comfortable for you?" she asked. Her breath hitched when she spoke, and I knew she was getting turned on, just like me.

Instead of answering her, I placed my hands on her bare thighs and slowly smoothed them up the length of her legs until I reached her shorts. Working their way over her shorts, my palms cupped her round ass, and in one quick movement, I pulled her closer to me so that my hard-on was pressed against the inside of her thigh. She gasped when she felt it.

"Now what, Charlie?" I growled.

She gulped. "Now, you kiss me."

She didn't have to tell me twice. Wrapping my arms around her waist, I pulled her to me and crashed my lips onto hers. Like before, there was nothing gentle about this kiss. Our tongues swirled together, and our mouths only parted long enough to take a breath of air. Her hands tugged on my hair, and she began slowly grinding her pelvis against my raging hard-on.

"Brody, touch me," she moaned against my mouth.

I slid my hands under the front of her shirt and cupped her breasts in each palm. She was wearing a bra, but I could feel her puckered nipples through the thin fabric and massaged them with my thumbs. When she moaned again, I nearly flipped her onto her back and took her right there.

Suddenly, a door slammed open and we both froze. It was after business hours on a Saturday, very few people were in the building to begin with. Who would be wandering around at this hour?

"Someone's coming," Charlie whispered.

I listened carefully and heard a female voice coming from the far end of the room. It was gradually getting louder, and whoever it was, they were getting closer. We both shot to our feet and went to make it look like we had been cleaning.

"Yes, for the love of God, I'm alone." It was Camila's voice we heard, and it sounded as though she was having a heated conversation with someone on the phone. "Roman had an off-site dinner meeting, he's not here anymore. I'm on the IT floor right now."

"Quick, get in the men's bathroom," I said under my breath. Charlie did as I told her, and we pressed our ears to the door once we were inside.

"I told you, there are more security measures in place since Roman discovered the breach. I can barely open a Word document without entering a million passwords." There was a brief pause while she listened to whatever the person on the other line had to say. "I'm doing the best I can!" She screamed into the phone. She cleared her throat and spoke quieter, "I'm going to need more time. These computers are fingerprint protected … if I can get him drunk tonight, there's a good chance he'll spill some info."

Charlie and I exchanged a confused look.

Who the hell was she talking to?

"I know what's at stake," Camila continued. We heard her footsteps again, this time she was coming towards the restrooms. She was nearly outside the door when we heard her say: "I will figure something out—hang on."

There was a long pause, and Charlie and I held our breath while we waited to be discovered—the cleaning cart was right outside the door after all.

"I need to go," she finally said. "I don't think I'm alone anymore … I'll take care of whoever it is."

Assuming she ended the call, her footsteps picked up again, slower than before, but then stopped right outside the girl's bathroom. We heard the door creak open, and her heels clicked a few times on the linoleum as she stepped in.

"I know one of you is around here," she said to no one in particular.

It would only be a matter of seconds before she opened the men's room and found us here. Neither of us was brave enough to move, fearing we would make too much noise. The women's bathroom door swung shut, and I held Charlie close in anticipation.

While we listened for the sounds of her footsteps, we heard the ding of the elevator instead.

"There you are!" Another female voice said. "Roman has been trying to get a hold of you. I told him I'd see if you were still here."

"Angela, how many times do I have to tell you?" Camila barked. Her footsteps marched towards the sound of the other woman, and Charlie and I both let out the breath we had been holding. "If I don't answer his calls, I am clearly busy. Did you not tell him this?"

The elevator doors promptly closed, and we didn't hear the woman's response.

"What do you think that was about?" Charlie asked when I released my hold on her.

"I don't know, but it was definitely strange." I opened the bathroom door and stuck my head out to make sure Camila was actually gone. When the coast was clear, we stepped back into the hallway.

"Do you think she's trying to get some kind of information out of Roman?"

I scoffed. "Wouldn't put it past her. Probably isn't that hard either. Camila's got Roman wrapped around her finger."

"Maybe we should tell him what we heard," she suggested. "Maybe it's nothing, but if she has to get him drunk to talk, I feel like it's probably something important."

"No." I shook my head. "Let's leave them be. The last thing we need is to give them another reason to come after us."

She chewed on her lip as if she were stopping herself from arguing with me. "Fine, we'll let it go."

We got back to cleaning the bathrooms, and a few hours later we had finished every single one in the building. It was nearing ten o'clock, and I was exhausted. Between the swim clinic and all of this cleaning, it had been a very long day.

Charlie and I hadn't talked much after we overheard Camila's conversation. I was still trying to process what we had heard, and I expected Charlie was still wanting to tell Roman. She didn't say anything more about it though, so maybe she did in fact decide to forget about it.

Before we left, we grabbed our belongings from the cleaning cart and made our way to the lobby. I checked my phone and noticed I had four missed calls from Landon. He never called me this much.

Something must have happened.

"Do you still want to come over to my place?" Charlie asked, unaware of my sudden panic.

I was about to answer her when my phone started ringing again and Landon's name popped up on my screen. "Hold on just a sec," I told Charlie. "What's up, Landon? Is everything okay?" I asked when I answered.

"Where are you?" he asked immediately. I could hear the fear in his voice, and I knew something was up.

"I'm at Howard Enterprises. Why? What's going on?"

"It's my dad. He's very upset, and I think he's drunk too. I had to get out of there." I heard him breathing heavily on the other end of the phone and wondered if he had been running.

"Where did you go? I'm about to leave, I can come get you," I told him. I motioned for Charlie to follow me back to the main door so I could get going as soon as I got off the phone.

"I'm outside your house," Landon said. "I ran here. I've been here for a while, can you hurry?"

"Yeah, I'm on my way. I'll be there in a few." I hung up the phone and turned to Charlie. We were alone in the lobby, and the only light was one security light that dimly lit the room. "Charlie, I'm sorry, but something has come up with Landon. As much as I'd love to come over, I have to be there for him tonight."

"Is everything okay?" she asked, a worried expression on her face.

"It's a really long story." I shook my head. "Rain check?"

"Yeah, that's fine, I understand," she said.

Placing my hand on the back of her head, I pulled her into me for one more kiss. "I'll see you on Monday."

She nodded, and I turned and darted out the door to my car. My house was probably a good twenty minutes away, but I pushed the speed limit and was able to get there in less than fifteen. When I pulled into my driveway, I could barely make out the shape of Landon's body huddled in my doorway.

Getting out of my car, I ran up to the door. "Landon, you okay, man? What happened?"

He looked up, but in the dark, it was hard to read his expression. "Can we go inside?" he asked.

I unlocked the door and ushered him in. "Tell me what happened." I turned the lights on and locked the door again once we were both inside.

"I'm not even entirely sure." He shook his head. "We had finished dinner, and he said he needed to make a phone call. I was just about done washing the dishes and cleaning everything up, when he came into the kitchen and started throwing things around the room. He had been drinking, too. I'm assuming the phone call must not have gone very well."

"Did you hear any of the conversation?" I asked.

"No, he went downstairs into his study."

"Did he say anything while he was throwing shit around?"

He shrugged. "Just swore a bunch. Said something about not being able to rely on anybody. But things got out of hand in a hurry. I asked him several times to stop, and he just kept on going. When he pushed me across the room, I crawled to the front door, tried to avoid getting hit by flying objects, and made a break for it. I couldn't tell if he was mad at me, or if it was something else. I didn't look to see if he followed me."

"Did you get hurt?" I took a quick glance over his body but didn't see any immediate signs of injuries.

He held onto his shoulder with the opposite hand, but shook his head no.

"Are you lying to me?" I asked, taking a step closer.

"No." He turned the shoulder he was clutching away from me, and I knew he was hiding something.

I jumped for his arm and was able to lift his sleeve up to get a better look. On his shoulder was a massive bruise. It had to be nearly the size of a baseball, and it was a very dark shade of purple already. "Jesus, Landon. Did you land on your arm, or did he hit you with something?"

"I don't even remember," he sighed. "It all happened so fast."

"Can you move it okay?"

"For now, but I don't know how it's going to feel in the morning."

"I'll get you ice and some ibuprofen." I went to my kitchen to get the supplies. "Then you need to lay down and get some sleep. Hopefully, you'll feel better in the morning."

"Brody, I'm scared." He said it so quietly I almost didn't catch it.

I turned around to face him again, but his head was down so I couldn't see his face. Walking back to him, I placed a hand on his good shoulder and gave it a squeeze. "I know, man. Do we need to call the police?"

His head shot up, and his eyes were filled with unshed tears. "No, I couldn't do that to my dad."

"Landon, he's done much worse to you—"

"I know, but it feels wrong. He's the only family I have."

I nodded. "Okay, I get it. If you change your mind, though, I'll be there for you. You don't have to go through this alone."

He wrapped his arms around me for a hug, and for a moment, I didn't know how to react. He'd never hugged me before.

"Thanks, Brody."

Patting his shoulder, I couldn't help but smile. "I got you, brother."

Chapter Fourteen

Charlie

In the days that followed the swim clinic, I fell into my new swim/work routine with ease. The number of days before my first swim meet became fewer and fewer, and I grew more excited—and a little nervous—the closer it got. The swim workouts had become much more intense, but Coach Tanner finally agreed to give us a short taper for the meet. The yardage we swam was decreased over the last few days, and he eliminated the weight sessions altogether.

It was now the Thursday before we would leave for Atlanta, and I was finishing some things up at work. I kept glancing at the clock, praying time would move faster so I could get out of here. I had plans with Brody tonight, and it was the first time we would have the chance to be alone since the night at Howard Enterprises.

Every night since then, Landon had been staying at Brody's house. Brody and I would have dinner together, but then I'd leave afterwards so the two guys could spend time together before crashing for the night. From the little I've heard about Landon's home life, it was hard to be upset that I had no alone time with Brody, but at the same time, Brody and I were kind of an item now. I wanted him to make time for me, too. Fortunately, Landon was planning to stay with a friend tonight, so we'd finally have some time to ourselves.

Snapping myself back to the present, I looked down at the monthly schedule I was formulating, and willed myself not to look at the clock again until I was finished.

However, as soon as I got started, another distraction came knocking, and I looked up to see Allison standing in the doorway.

"Hey, I've got a few minutes to kill before I need to go back to the pool. Was wondering if you had time to chat?" she asked. I waved her in, and she took a seat in the chair across from my desk.

"What's up?" I asked, setting my work to the side.

"Just me being nosy, I suppose," she giggled. "I've been waiting ever so patiently for you to give me the deets on how things are going between you and Brody! But, my patience has run out, so here I am." She splayed her arms out in front of her to emphasize her presence, and I couldn't help but laugh.

"Sorry, I totally wasn't trying to keep you in the dark. There hasn't been much to tell, unfortunately."

She frowned. "What do you mean? I see you guys talking all the time. *Something* has to have happened."

"I mean, yeah, we talk all the time. We have dinner together most evenings, but that's about it." I shrugged one of my shoulders. "Things got pretty steamy at Howard Enterprises, but nothing has happened since then."

"Oh, hold up!" She sat up straighter. "You didn't tell me that!"

I laughed. "Well, I haven't told anyone if it makes you feel any better."

"Maybe a little." She laughed. "But nothing has happened since? That was almost two weeks ago."

"I know." I made a face. "Landon has been staying with Brody every night since then. The opportunity just hasn't been there with him around."

"Any idea what's going on with that?"

"Not really," I said, shaking my head. "The night we were at Howard Enterprises, Brody just told me it was a long story. He hasn't said anything about it though, and I don't want to press the issue, so I haven't asked."

"I can understand that." She nodded slowly. "But at the same time, if something serious is going on, he needs to tell someone. Maybe one of us could help them in some way."

"There's also the possibility Landon asked him not to tell anyone, though."

"I also get that, but if you two are going to be in a relationship, he should at least give you *some* details, right?" She paused for me to answer but continued when I stayed silent. "I don't know, maybe I'm wrong, but if I was in your situation, I'd be getting a little frustrated."

I scoffed. "Oh, trust me, I am getting a little frustrated. But at the same time, it's hard to be mad at him for doing the right thing."

"He can do the right thing *and* make time for his girlfriend," she said. "He doesn't have to pick one or the other."

Before I could respond, we heard Mr. Davis yelling from inside his office. The walls were usually pretty good at keeping sounds out, so we knew he was upset if we could hear him.

"What's he doing here?" Allison whispered. "I thought he usually bounced once your shift started."

I nodded. "He usually does. He's rarely here when I am. I wonder what's got him so riled up."

We listened for a minute, but it was hard to make out full sentences: "We are out of time ... need more ... whatever it takes, Camila."

"Camila?" Both Allison and I said at the same time.

"Camila Hale?" Allison repeated. "As in, Roman's Camila?"

"How many other Camila's could there be?" I shrugged.

"I didn't know they knew each other."

"Maybe it's something swimming related," I suggested. "Could he just be trying to get Landon more sponsors or something?"

"Yeah, maybe that's it."

We listened for a few moments more, but Mr. Davis had gone quiet, and we assumed his conversation had ended.

"Anyway." I shook my head and re-gathered my paperwork. "I need to get some work done. What are we doing about wine night tomorrow?"

Our wine and pizza night was now a regular thing, and I looked forward to it every week. But this Friday we would be in Atlanta for the swim meet.

"Your parents are coming down for the meet, aren't they?" She stood from her chair and started for the door of my office, lingering in the doorway as she awaited my response.

"Yes, they'll arrive about the same time we will tomorrow, and then they are leaving Saturday evening. It'll be a quick trip for them."

"My parents are coming, too. We should take them all out to dinner. We can still have wine." She winked.

I smiled. "Sounds good to me. Text me tonight, we can plan something later." I waved to her, and she blew me an air kiss as she disappeared from my office.

My shoulders sagged once she was out of view as I thought about Brody again. I didn't want to overstep any boundaries by sticking my nose where it didn't belong, but Allison had made a good point: I *did* deserve to know what was going on. Maybe not everything, but enough to put my mind at ease. I'd talk to him tonight and get to the bottom of whatever was going on.

Chapter Fifteen

Brody

"Wow, you look beautiful," I told Charlie when I opened the door. She was wearing a floral sundress with sandals, and her long hair flowed down her back. "Please, come in."

"Thank you." She blushed. She stopped a few steps in. "I see you still haven't had time to clean up your living room," she teased. The usual mess of dirty dishes and food wrappers littered the floor and furniture.

"Are you and Landon ganging up on me, now?" I laughed as I closed the door. "I'll get around to it." I took her in my arms, smoothing her hair back with one hand, and pulling her closer with the other. "I'm glad we finally have some time to be alone."

"Me too," she breathed.

Her gaze didn't leave my lips, and I knew she wanted me to kiss her. Smiling, I backed her up against the door and pressed my lips against hers. It didn't take long for her to open for me, and soon our tongues were swirling together with passion. She had her arms around my neck and her fingers tugged at my hair. I made a trail of kisses along her jaw and down to her neck, tasting the sweetness of her skin.

Feeling brave, I let my hands drop to her thighs, and inched them higher beneath the hem of her dress. I smoothed my fingers along her naked flesh until I reached the softness of her cotton panties. Ever since I first laid eyes on Charlie, I dreamed of running my hands over her perfectly round ass, and I couldn't resist giving it a hard squeeze.

"Brody," she gasped.

Tucking my thumbs in to the waistband of her underwear, I attempted to slide them down her legs, but she held my hands in place.

"Brody," she said again.

I stopped kissing her neck and met her gaze. "I'm sorry." Immediately dropping my hands to my sides, I took half a step back. "I got carried away. That was too far."

She giggled and gave me a quick peck on the lips. "It's not that I don't want that." The desire still sparked in her eyes, and it took a lot of self-control not to kiss her again. "I've been wanting to talk to you about something, and I'd just like to clear some things up before we go any further."

I frowned. That didn't sound good.

"Is everything okay?" I asked her.

She nodded towards the kitchen. "Is dinner ready? We can talk while we eat."

My stomach dropped as unease filled me. "Uh, yeah. I made some spaghetti." I took her hand in mine, and she let me lead her into the kitchen.

"It smells good!" She smiled.

After loading up both of our plates with pasta and garlic toast, we sat at the table across from each other. Charlie dug into her spaghetti right away, while I stared at my plate. I suddenly wasn't hungry, and I wasn't going to relax until she told me what was going on.

"So, what did you want to talk to me about?" I asked, unable to wait any longer.

She set her fork down and sighed. "I've been thinking a lot about that night at Howard Enterprises."

A smile tugged at the corner of my mouth. "I think about that night a lot, too."

She didn't return my smile. "The problem is, that we haven't had any alone time since then."

"It's not like we don't see each other every day," I argued. "We've both been busy. You with work, and I've had a lot of photoshoots popping up recently."

"I know, but in the evenings, we have time, and you hang out with Landon instead." She stared at her plate as she spoke. "I guess I just don't understand why you have time for him, but not for me."

I rolled my eyes. Now I was just getting impatient. "Charlie, Landon is going through some shit right now. He needs someone to be there for him. I'm not going to apologize for being a good friend."

"I don't expect you to." Her head snapped up and she glared at me. "I'm just saying that we've had the opportunity to have alone time, and you choose not to take it. It's frustrating when I walk in

132

here, and the first thing you say is that you're so glad we *finally* have some alone time. Like it's *my* fault we haven't been able to get together."

"What do you want me to say, Charlie?" I asked, throwing my hands up in frustration. "You want me to leave Landon high and dry? Tell him to figure it out on his own?"

"Don't be ridiculous, you know that's not what I meant!" She was upset now. The glare was still in place, but her voice wavered slightly as though she were fighting the urge to cry. "You told me that night you would tell me what's going on. I respected that, so I haven't pushed. But now I want to know. What's so important that you can't be there for us both?"

"Landon doesn't have a good home life," I said, trying to keep my voice level.

"I already know that."

"Then what else is there to say?" I argued. "Shouldn't that be a good enough reason to want to be there for someone?"

"But what's changed in the last couple of weeks? If he's always had it tough at home, then why are you suddenly spending so much more time with him *now*?"

"He's afraid to go home, and he has no other family!" I practically shouted at her, and the volume of my voice made her jump. "Heaven forbid I want to be there for him."

She crossed her arms and sat back in her seat. Her lip started to tremble as she struggled to keep her tears at bay. After a long stretch of silence, she finally reached forward and took a sip of water before she spoke again. "I have no family out here either, Brody."

My face softened a touch. "It's different—"

"Yeah, it is different." She nodded. "But, it's still lonely. I need you too, and I shouldn't have to fight for your time and attention."

I didn't know what to say, so I remained silent. She had a point, but so did I. Landon was still a kid, he needed someone to look out for him.

A few moments of silence passed, and she must have grown tired of waiting for me to say something. She threw her napkin on the table, and the legs of her chair scraped the floor as she pushed it back and stood up.

"Where are you going?" My stomach plummeted further. I was mad, but I didn't want her to leave either.

"I'm going home," she said as she stomped her way out of the kitchen. After a few steps, she stopped and spun on her heel to face me. "Think about it, Brody. I'm not going to be the one putting in all the effort. If you want a relationship with me, I need to see something coming from you, too." A moment later, the door slammed shut, and she was gone.

Maybe I should have gone after her, but I had nothing to say. I saw her and talked to her every day, why couldn't she be happy with that? Why did women have to be so damn needy? I shoved my plate away from me. I was no longer hungry.

Instead, I picked up my keys off the counter and walked out the door. I didn't feel like sitting at home by myself, and I wanted a beer. There was a dingy little bar only a couple of miles from my house, so I pulled in there.

It shouldn't have surprised me that it was busy, it was Thursday night after all. The place was packed with young adults standing around in small groups, some were dancing to the loud pop music that was playing over the speakers, others were throwing back rounds of shots. I tried shoving my way through the crowd when one woman, whose outfit was clearly too small for her, tried grinding up on me.

"Hey, what's your name?" she purred in my ear.

Instead of responding, I gently peeled her off of me and kept walking to the dimly lit bar. Soon after I ordered a drink and sat down, someone came calling my name.

"I thought that looked like Brody Hayes!" A pair of arms wrapped around my shoulders and shook me so hard I nearly fell out of my chair. I didn't see who the voice belonged to right away, but I didn't need to.

"Chase, chill out, you're going to knock me to the ground." I used my hands to balance myself against the bar, and then resituated myself when Chase released his hold.

"Man, I was coming over here to beat your ass for getting all over my girl," he slurred, pointing to the scantily dressed woman that had been grinding up on me a minute ago. "But then I realized it was you!" He then pointed his finger at me, lost this balance, and I had to grab his hand and steady him before he poked my eye out.

"Dude, I have no interest in your lady," I said. "How much have you had to drink?"

"What's it to you?" He yelled. If it wasn't for the loud music, I'm sure he would have turned some heads. "We aren't friends anymore, remember?"

I sighed. "Chase, you're a bad influence on me. If I get into any more trouble, I'll risk my swimming career. You get that, right?"

"Yeah, yeah. Swimming, shwimming." He rocked back and forth before finally taking a seat on the barstool next to me. "So, why are you here, then? Shouldn't you be at home like a good boy?"

I rolled my eyes and took a sip of my beer before I answered. "I'm having lady troubles. I needed to get out of the house for a bit."

"You?" Chase pointed at me again. "Lady troubles? Psh, forget her. We can find you someone better."

"I don't know if there is anyone better than her," I said, more to myself than to Chase.

"I know a lot of girls," Chase continued as though he didn't hear me. "What are you looking for? Oh, I know. Emma would be good for you. She's a bit crazy, but you definitely won't be disappointed, if ya know what I mean." He nudged me with his elbow. "Let me bring her over here."

I turned back to my drink, praying Chase was drunk enough that he wouldn't remember to come back over here. I didn't want another one-night stand. It didn't appeal to me like it used to.

I only wanted Charlie.

Maybe I did mess up tonight. She literally only wanted to spend some alone time together, which I would admit, I wasn't very good about. I was so concerned about looking out for Landon, that I forgot my own girlfriend needed someone to be there for her, too.

Throwing back the rest of my drink, I set a couple of bills on the counter and stood up to head out. I needed to call Charlie and apologize. Maybe I could still see her tonight and talk to her in person.

As I turned for the door, Chase returned with a tall, skinny red-head, who I assumed had to be Emma. She had more clothes on than the other girl, but not by much. Her skin-tight jeans and tube top left very little to the imagination.

"Brody, this is Emma," Chase said when they had reached me. Neither one of them could stand up straight without swaying back and forth. "I told her you were looking for a good time, and she's down to hang."

Emma took a few more shaken steps towards me and flung her arms around my neck. "You want to get out of here?" she whispered into my ear. She was so close I could feel the heat of her breath on my neck, and the next thing I knew, she was nipping at my flesh with her teeth.

"Nope, I don't think so." Taking her arms in mine, I lifted them away from me and held her at arm's length. Instead of responding, she stuck her lip out and pouted.

"What the hell, man?" Chase asked.

He slipped an arm around Emma's waist, pulled her close to him, and whispered something in her ear. She shot me one more lustful glance and disappeared back into the crowd.

I went for the exit once more, but Chase cut me off. "What, are you too good to accept my help now?"

"That kind of stuff doesn't interest me anymore." I shrugged. "Plus, I have a girlfriend now."

He laughed. "So? You were obviously having issues or you wouldn't have come here tonight. I say, screw her. We'll find you someone better, doesn't have to be Emma."

"I said no, Chase."

"Come on, man. I'm trying to help you. We'll show that bitch—"

"Do *not* call Charlie a bitch," I said through clenched teeth. Chase was dangerously close to me losing my shit. "I'm not going to cheat on her. Goodbye, Chase." I took my phone out of my pocket and pulled up Charlie's number. Taking a step around Chase, I attempted to make my way to the exit a third time, when suddenly, my phone was ripped out of my hand.

I whipped back around to face Chase. "What the fuck—" My mouth dropped open when he plunged my phone into someone else's drink. Soaking the entire thing.

"Fuck you and your problems, Brody," Chase spat at me.

Without thinking, I threw back my arm and punched him right between the eyes. He fell to the ground with a loud thud, and those standing around us all turned their attention in our direction. Chase brought his hand to his head and yelled several expletives as a few of his lady friends gathered around him.

"Hey, you!" The muscular bouncer that let me in, grabbed me by the back of the shirt. "Get out of here, or I'll call the cops."

I held my hands up in surrender. "I was leaving anyway. Can I have my phone?"

The guy who was holding the drink with my phone in it fished it out and tossed it to me as the bouncer led me outside. Once I had stepped out of the bar, I checked to see if it was still working, but it wouldn't even light up.

Clenching my fists, I let my head fall back so that I was staring at the dark sky. "Seriously, could this day get any worse?"

Trudging back to my car, I threw my dead phone onto the empty passenger seat and made my way home. When I arrived a few minutes later, I noticed through the front window that the lights were on, even though I was pretty certain I had turned them all off before I left. More than likely Landon had used the spare key I gave him to get inside, but he was supposed to be at a friend's house tonight.

Walking up to my front door, I opened it and cautiously stuck my head inside. "Landon? Are you here?"

"In here," he called from the kitchen.

Letting out a breath, I followed the sound of his voice and found him sitting at the table surrounded by a pile of papers. "What are you doing here?" I asked him. "I thought you were staying with a friend tonight?"

"I was, but he didn't feel very good after we ate, so I tried to go home. There's something I need to tell you. I think my dad might have had something to do with the breach at Howard Enterprises."

Chapter Sixteen

Landon

"Sorry again that Ethan wasn't feeling very well tonight," Mrs. Fuller said as she pulled up to my house. "We'll have you over again soon."

"It's no problem." I stepped out of the vehicle. "Thanks for driving me home."

"Take care, Landon!" She waved and then I shut the car door and turned to go inside my house. The lights were on, and I could hear voices the closer I got to the door. Clearly, my dad had someone over. Maybe I should have asked to be dropped off at Brody's instead.

Sighing, I opened the door and snuck inside as quietly as I could. If I could just slip off to my room without my dad hearing—

"Landon?" he growled from the kitchen. "Is that you?" There was some mumbling I couldn't quite make out, the sound of shuffling papers drowned out most of it, anyway.

I froze to my spot. Would he be angry that I'm here? "Yeah, It-it's me," I finally said.

He came into the living room and crossed his arms when he saw me. "What are you doing home? I thought you'd be out tonight."

"That was the original plan." I nodded. "Ethan got sick, so his mom dropped me off."

"Well, I'll give you twenty minutes to make other arrangements," he huffed. "I'm still working, and I don't need you in the way. Victor, let's take this outside until the kid is gone."

A short, dark-haired Hispanic man that I didn't recognize came into view. He had a black duffel bag flung over his shoulder and was wearing jeans and a dark t-shirt. "Where do you want this, boss?" he asked my dad, holding up the bag.

"Put it in my study for now, we'll come back to it."

My dad's study was in the basement, and since I was standing in front of the staircase, Victor had to walk right by me on his way down.

"Are you a new employee of my dad's?" I asked him. "I don't recognize you." I obviously didn't know all of my dad's employees,

138

but I had been to the gym enough times to know who most of them were.

Victor came to a halt in front of me but didn't respond. Instead, he looked to my dad as if he were unsure of what to say.

"It's none of your concern, Landon." In two steps, my dad was standing in front of me and took me by the collar of my shirt. "Just get whatever shit you need and find somewhere else to go tonight. You're wasting our time." He let me go and glared after me as I went to my room to get my stuff.

I tried calling Brody to see if he could come get me, but the call went straight to voicemail, so I ordered an Uber. Unfortunately, the closest car was a good fifteen minutes away. Hopefully, my dad could be a little patient. He was clearly already in a mood, and I didn't want to make it worse.

What was going on out there with this Victor guy, anyway? My dad's gym was open 24/7, it's not like they couldn't do business from there. And what was in that duffel bag? My dad had Victor put it in his study, probably because he knows that I know his study is off-limits. Did he think I was going to go snooping?

Well, now I was curious. Something smelled a little fishy, and I wanted to find out. I still had eleven minutes before my Uber was to arrive, so I grabbed my backpack, stuck my head out my bedroom door, and crept down the hall when I didn't hear any voices. Peering around the corner, I could see my dad and Victor through the window leading to our patio. They were each smoking a cigar with their backs facing me. If I stayed low to the ground, I could probably get to the basement without either of them seeing me.

Getting down on all fours, I crawled to the base of the stairs, never taking my eyes off the window. When I reached the first step, my dad turned around to look inside, and I immediately sank as far into the floor as I could. Holding my breath, I prayed he wouldn't see me. A moment later, Victor pointed to something across the yard, and my dad's attention was directed away from the window. I let out the breath I had been holding and quickly descended the rest of the staircase.

My dad's study was right at the bottom of the stairs, and luckily—for me—Victor hadn't locked the door after he dropped off the duffel bag. Pushing open the door, I went into the study for the first time ever. I'm not really sure what I was expecting, but what I found wasn't it.

The room was dimly lit by a single lamp sitting in the corner and smelled of cigar smoke and old books. A bookcase took up the entirety of one of the walls and was filled to the brim with books and filing folders. On the other side of the room, at least half a dozen filing cabinets were lined up next to each other, each of them taller than I was. I pulled at one of the drawers, but it was locked.

I desperately wanted to explore the room further, but it was only a matter of minutes before my dad could come back inside and find me.

After a quick scan of the room, I found Victor's duffel bag sitting on the chair by the desk. Going straight for that, I ripped it open and began pulling out the contents: a pair of jeans and a red sweater, a couple of folders, and at the bottom of the bag sat several handguns.

"Oh, shit." Caught off guard, I dropped the bag back onto the chair with a thud. Freezing to my spot, I waited to hear the sound of the door opening and my dad fumbling down the stairs, but the sounds never came.

Setting the guns aside, I flipped open one of the folders to find several bank deposit slips. They were written in Spanish, so I couldn't read a lot of the writing, but the currency was in American Dollars, and each one totaled well over a thousand dollars. I could understand enough of the document to realize all the money had been transferred from the same place: Howard Enterprises.

My mouth dropped open, and for a moment, I was so in shock, I didn't know what to do. I was brought out of my trance when my phone buzzed, notifying me that my Uber had arrived.

Not sure what else to do, I shoved the folders into my backpack and scurried back up the stairs. I was reaching for the door, when my dad and Victor came bursting back in.

"Is that your car?" my dad asked.

"Yep, going to Brody's house." As soon as I said it, I regretted doing so. If they noticed the folders were missing tonight, they'd know exactly where to find me.

"Good, I'll come get the both of you to head to the airport tomorrow," my dad added before I had reached the car door. "If you're not ready by eleven, we're not going. And I won't be happy."

I nodded and got into the car, telling the driver to go. I didn't even care if I was being rude, I just wanted him to move.

Brody hadn't answered his phone when I tried to call him, and I knew he was having Charlie over tonight. I'm sure he'd be less than thrilled when I showed up uninvited, but I couldn't wait. We had to discuss this tonight.

When I reached his house, none of the lights were on, and I soon realized he wasn't home. Luckily, he had given me a spare key for instances such as this, and I let myself in. I tried calling him again to give him a heads up and ask where he was at, but it went straight to voicemail again.

Hoping he wouldn't be gone long, I took the folders out of my backpack and sorted the papers out to study them a little closer. Based on these receipts, it was clear that my dad and that Victor guy had taken the money out of one Howard Enterprise's accounts. But where had he put it?

I picked up one of the receipts, and skimmed through the entire document, looking for a sign as to where the money went. Unfortunately, I didn't understand Spanish, and I couldn't make out most of what it said.

However, one particular sentence stuck out to me: *¡Gracias por realizar operaciones bancarias con nosotros, Landon Davis!*

"Why the hell is my name on this?" I took my phone out of my pocket, pulled up Google translate, and entered the phrase into the box. It said: *Thank you for banking with us, Landon Davis!*

My heart plummeted, and I suddenly felt sick. Not only was my dad smuggling money—he was depositing it into an account under *my name*.

This shit just kept getting worse.

Chapter Seventeen

Charlie

I checked my phone one final time before I switched it to airplane mode for our flight to Atlanta, but still no word from Brody. A little while after I had gotten home last night, I tried calling him to apologize for how I handled the situation, but he didn't answer. We didn't have practice this morning because of the meet starting tonight, so I didn't even have the chance to talk to him in person. I was starting to think he was angry with me, and I hoped I didn't ruin my chances with him.

"Still haven't heard anything?" Allison asked from the seat next to me. I had explained everything to her on the ride to the airport.

"No, and I'm starting to get a little worried," I sighed and shoved my phone into my carry-on.

She reached over and squeezed my arm. "I'm sure there's a good reason why he hasn't gotten back to you. Maybe he fell asleep and he isn't up yet. His flight *is* later than ours."

"Yeah, maybe that's it." I turned to look out the window as we started moving away from the gate.

The flight was only about an hour long, and I tried to catch a small nap, but couldn't seem to relax my mind enough to fall asleep. I didn't sleep well last night either because I kept thinking about why Brody wasn't answering his phone. The same thought was haunting my mind now, and I couldn't shake it from my head no matter how hard I tried.

Not surprisingly, the flight ended all too quickly, and I didn't manage to get any sleep by the time we landed in Atlanta. Allison passed out almost right away, and she stirred in her seat once we touched the ground.

"We here already?" she mumbled, stretching her arms out in front of her. "Did you get any sleep?"

"Yes, we're here, but no, I didn't sleep." I shrugged. "Could just be from the nerves of my first meet."

She nodded but didn't look entirely convinced. "Yeah, it could be."

When we got off the plane, neither of us had checked any baggage, but we made our way to the baggage claim anyway. My parents were due to arrive any minute, and I told them we would wait for them there. Allison and I settled onto a bench, and I pulled my phone out to scroll through my feeds until I heard someone calling out my name.

"Charlie! Is that you?"

I looked up and saw my mom running through the airport towards me. I stood up just as she crashed into me with a huge hug. "Hi Mom!" I hugged her close, missing her embrace.

After what happened with Brody last night, I considered calling her and talking to her about it, but ultimately decided not to. I knew I'd be seeing her today, anyway, and I had secretly hoped Brody would have gotten back to me long before I saw her.

"I've missed you so much, darling." She held me at arm's length so she could inspect me thoroughly. "Those swim workouts are doing wonders for you!"

"Now, dear, it's been less than a month since we've seen her. She doesn't look *that* different," my dad chuckled as he leaned in to give me a hug. "It's good to see you, squirt. Been a few days since we've heard from you."

"Good to see you too, Dad." I squeezed my eyes tight when I hugged him, soaking up all the love my parents had to offer. "I've been kind of busy the last few days and haven't had a chance to call," I said after pulling away from my dad. "But, let me introduce you to my teammate. Mom, Dad, this is Allison. She's one of my closest friends in Jacksonville."

"It's so wonderful to meet you." Allison smiled as she shook hands with both of my parents. "Charlie has told me so many wonderful things about you both."

"Same to you, Allison," my mom said smiling. "I understand your parents are coming up for the meet this weekend as well. Are they to arrive soon? We can wait for them here if you'd like?"

"Yes, they are coming, but they decided to drive instead of fly. My dad isn't a huge fan of airplanes," Allison said. "They won't be here for another hour or so and said they would just meet us at the pool."

"Very good! Shall we go get checked in to our hotel?" My mom clapped her hands together and led us out the doors where she hailed a cab.

We spent the entire drive catching up on events over the last few weeks and reminiscing old memories. Of course, my parents had to tell Allison about several embarrassing moments I had growing up, and we were in a fit of giggles by the time we arrived at our hotel.

Once we were all checked in to our respective rooms, we gathered in my room to hang out for a bit before we had to go to the pool. My mom and I were sitting together on the bed, while Allison and my dad sat on opposite ends of the couch.

"So, Charlie," my mom said after a while. "When do we get to meet Brody? Sounds like you two may be getting pretty serious. I'm so glad you decided to give him a chance."

I shrugged. "Oh, I'm sure he'll be at the pool this evening."

Brody did finally send me a message when we were leaving the airport, but all it said was: 'Leaving Jacksonville, see you in a bit.' No explanation as to why he never called me back last night, or why he never tried to call me anytime this morning. I was a little irritated with him, and I didn't want my parents to suspect that anything was wrong.

"Have you heard back from him yet, Charlie?" Allison asked.

"Yes, he's on the plane." I shot her a glance, and she picked up the hint and didn't ask anything more about him.

"Oh, I can't wait to meet him!" my mom squealed, clearly not noticing the exchange between Allison and me.

"Tell us a little bit more about him," my dad said. "I've only gotten bits and pieces. What's he like?"

"He's nice." I nodded. I realized it was a vague answer, but I still wasn't sure where we stood after last night. I didn't want to get them excited if Brody decided we were over.

My dad chuckled. "He's nice? That's all you can say about him?"

"He has a unique personality that's difficult to describe," Allison said, jumping to my rescue. "You'll just have to meet him."

"Well, what are we waiting for?" My mom jumped up from the bed. "Let's get going!"

Mouthing *thank you* to Allison, I got up and gathered my things to head to the pool.

Warmups weren't until 5:30, so we still had over an hour before we needed to get in the water, but I was anxious to get going. Brody sent me another text as we were headed out the door that they had landed, and I knew they wouldn't be far behind us.

Once we were at the pool, we found Coach Tanner was already there and had set up a little designated spot for all of us in the stands. Sometimes being early had its perks, as our spot was closest to the stairs to give us easy access to the pool. He waved us over, and soon he and my parents were deep in conversation while Allison and I got ready for warmups.

At some point while we were changing, Allison's parents showed up, and she ran over to greet them as soon as she saw them. She was the spitting image of both of her parents. She had her mom's blonde hair, her dad's height, and a mixture of each of their facial features—like her dad's nose and her mom's eyes. It wasn't hard to tell they were related. Introductions were made, and as soon as I sat down after saying hello, I noticed Brody, Landon, and Mr. Davis making their way over to us.

"Mr. Davis, I'm glad you could join us!" Coach Tanner shook his hand when he approached. "Long time no see. I think this will be a good meet for Landon."

"I'm banking on it," Mr. Davis said. "I have high expectations for that kid."

They continued to chat as Brody and Landon made their way up the stairs to set up closer to Allison and me.

"Hey, Charlie," Brody said when he saw me. He was all smiles, as if last night had never happened. "Are these your parents?" He turned his attention to them. "I'm Brody Hayes. It's so nice to meet you." He shook hands with my father first, and then my mother, who both smiled as they said hello.

"Brody, nice to meet you," my dad said. "Charlie has told us all about you. I sincerely hope you are treating my daughter like the princess she is."

"Dad," I shot him a warning glance before I smiled sweetly—possibly a little *too* sweetly, but whatever—and turned my attention back to Brody. I snuck a peek over in Allison's direction, and her eyes were darting between Brody and me as if she were also waiting for an explanation.

145

"I'm sorry, Brody," my mom said as she slipped an arm around her husband's shoulders. "He's always playing the overprotective father. Charlie has said nothing but nice things about you." She smiled sweetly.

"No worries, Mrs. Price. I totally get it." He smiled at her and then started digging through his bag for his cap and goggles.

"Alright guys," Coach Tanner said. "Let's get down on deck and get in the pool before it gets too crowded." He started making his way down the stairs, followed closely by Landon and Allison. Brody was shortly behind them, and I stripped my shirt and shorts off down to my warmup suit, grabbed my cap and goggles, and hurried after him.

"Brody," I called when he was nearly halfway down the stairs. He stopped and waited for me to catch up to him. "Brody, I tried to call you. I know I left your house upset last night, but—"

He pulled me to the side once we were at the bottom of the stairs and cut me off mid-sentence. "We are going to talk about that, and I'm sorry I didn't call you back last night. It's a long story that involves my phone getting dunked in a glass of beer."

I tilted my head. "What?"

He shook his head. "I'll tell you later. Anyway, I wanted to talk to you last night about something else, but my phone wasn't dried out until this morning. By the time I went to call you back, Mr. Davis showed up at my house to take us to the airport."

"So, how did that prevent you from calling me?" I asked.

"Because Landon found proof that Mr. Davis is the one who breached Roman's company, and I couldn't tell you that with him around."

"What?" I practically shouted.

"Shhh!" Brody covered my mouth with his fingers. "Again, it's a long story, and I promise I'll tell you everything, but not here. We need to be somewhere private. Can I come to your room tonight?"

"I have dinner plans with my parents and Allison's family, but I suppose you could come over after."

"I'll text you, okay?"

I nodded. "Okay."

"Let's go warm up before Coach comes after us." He took my hand and gave it a squeeze before he turned towards the water, pulling his cap on tight over his head as he went. A moment later he jumped in the pool and blended in with the other swimmers.

I was in so much shock I couldn't move for a few moments. What the hell did he mean he had proof?

******

After warm ups, Allison and I went to the locker rooms to help each other squeeze into our too-tight tech suits. The less drag we had, the faster we would go. Unfortunately, these suits weren't particularly fun to get into. Putting the suit on was almost a workout on its own. By the time we were finished changing, the meet was already well underway.

Down on deck, Landon had just finished swimming his 200 Individual Medley, and Coach gave him a solid smack on the shoulder, seemingly pleased with his performance. He came in third in his heat, and went a 2:08.76, dropping two seconds off his personal best time. I stole a glance at Mr. Davis to see if he was pleased as well, but he just sat back in his chair with his hands folded over his stomach. His expression gave nothing away, and for all I knew, he might not have even watched the race.

I shook my head and redirected my attention back to the pool. Brody's heat was now behind the blocks, ready to start. I knew this was one of his best races, and we expected him to do well tonight. He had won the gold medal in the 200 Individual Medley at the Olympics, and Coach was getting him ready to repeat it at the next games.

A moment later, the buzzer sounded, and Brody's heat was off the blocks and in the water. Brody was a clear front runner, leading the pack by almost a full body length by the end of the first 50 meters. Watching Brody swim, I thought about how gifted he was with his swimming ability. He was so strong and smooth in the water. He looked as though he was going for a relaxing swim, while all the other men in the heat looked like they were starting to die out. As Brody pushed off the wall to start the last 50 meters, he had a dominant lead in the heat. The swimmer in second was now over a full body length behind him.

"Holy shit, he might actually break the world record." Allison grabbed onto my arm and shook it excitedly, never tearing her eyes from the pool.

We saw Coach Tanner jumping up and down like a mad man on the pool deck while he yelled at Brody to go faster. Brody was roughly halfway down the length of the pool with about 25 meters left when the clock turned 1:42. The current record was 1:54. It was going to be close.

"GO BRODY!" We cheered him on from the stands. We screamed for him as the clock ticked. We were on the edge of our seats for a nail-biting finish. The last ten seconds lasted a lifetime as we waited to see if he'd make it. When Brody finished into the wall, we all looked at the scoreboard to see what his final time was. He came in at 1:55.24, missing the world record by just over a second. We cheered again, shocked he had come as close as he did to breaking it.

"Oh, my goodness, that was so close!" Allison cried. "How cool would that have been to start the meet with *that*?"

"It would have been amazing, but that was still a great race," I said. "And at least he qualified for Olympic trials."

"He had already qualified for trials," Landon said as he rejoined the group. "He went a 1:58 back in February."

"Oh, that's right! I remember him mentioning that. Well, he dropped time and had an awesome race. He will get the record soon enough, I'm sure of it. You had a great swim, too, Landon."

He smiled. "Thanks."

When Brody finished cooling down from his race and came back upstairs to the group, wearing nothing but his racing jammer and a towel slung over his shoulder, he was showered with praises and high-fives.

"Nice job, Brody. You killed it, man." Landon gave him a pat on the back.

"Thanks, so did you," Brody said. "I bet you'll get the trials cut before the end of the year."

"Let's hope so," Landon said as he sat back down next to his dad.

Mr. Davis gave Brody a high five, and I watched as Landon's face fell. His dad still hadn't acknowledged his own race, and my heart went out for him.

Allison had already gone down to the pool to prepare for her race, but both of our parents gave Brody praises as he walked by them.

"Good job, Brody. That was fun to watch," I said as he approached.

He came to a stop in front of me and broke into a grin that stretched from one ear to the other. "Thank you, Charlie. That means more to me than you know."

I smiled back, and we stayed like that for a moment. As the silence stretched on between us, I felt the others staring, and I tore my gaze from Brody's. I moved to respond, but before I could, Allison's mother pointed to the blocks where her daughter's race was about to start.

Allison was competing in the 200 breaststroke tonight, and it was one of her best races—after all, she did have the American record. We cheered her on from our spot on the bleachers, and she had a very solid race. She finished right on her time, around 2:18, and just barely out-touched the girl in the lane next to her. It was another nail-biting finish, but in the end, Allison came out on top and managed to maintain her record.

If these first few events of the meet said anything, it said we were all going to have one hell of a good weekend.

My first race—the 200 backstroke—was coming up next, and I was starting to get nervous. This was the moment I had been working for my whole life. Of course, I wanted to do well, but even if I didn't, I was just thrilled that I had made it as far as I did.

"Hey," Brody reappeared next to me and wrapped an arm around my shoulders. "You ready for this?" He smiled and gave me a tight squeeze.

"I'm not going to lie, I'm pretty nervous," I chuckled and held out my hands. "See? I'm shaking."

He held me tighter. "You have nothing to be nervous about. You're going to crush it. Now, let's get down there and see how your first professional race goes."

******

By the time the meet ended for the night, it was already almost nine o'clock. It was getting dark outside, and I was exhausted. I swam two events tonight: the 200 freestyle and the 200 backstroke, and I thought they both went well. I was in the fast heat for the 200 back, and dropped a whopping three seconds off my best time for a time of 2:06.17, which qualified me for the Olympic trials. I missed the American record by less than two seconds but was the overall winner of the race, so I was thrilled nonetheless.

The 200 freestyle was my second and last race of the evening. I was in the slow heat and placed second, dropping a second off my best time for a new time of 2:02.65, and missing the trials cut by less than a second. I managed to place fourth overall, which I couldn't complain about.

I was over the moon that I was doing so well for my first professional meet. At the end of the night, when I stood on the podium to accept my first-place medal, I was so overwhelmed with emotions I nearly cried. All the hard work and dedication I had put into this sport for all these years was finally paying off.

I was also thankful that my parents were able to come all the way down to Atlanta for a short trip to share this moment with me. I couldn't have done it without their love and support from day one, and I felt like I owed them this win to express just how thankful I was.

"I'm proud of you, kiddo." My dad slipped his arm around my shoulders as we left the building. "You've worked hard for this, and it shows when you're in the pool."

"I believe someone told you not too long ago that you would do great out here. I wonder who that was?" My mom teased.

"I know you said that Mom," I laughed. "I just didn't think it would happen this fast!"

"Well, believe it, sweetie. Because you're on the fast track to a great swimming career." She took hold of my hand and gave it a squeeze.

I squeezed back. "I love you guys."

"We love you too, Charlie," my dad said. "Now, let's go meet up with Allison's family and get something to eat, and then go to bed so you're energized for tomorrow."

"I can't wait." I smiled.

I was truly excited to spend some time with my family and get to know Allison's family as well, but part of me was also anxious for the night to be over so I could see Brody and find out what the hell was going on.

Chapter Eighteen

Brody

It was almost midnight by the time Charlie finally texted me back saying I could come over, but I didn't care. I needed to talk to her. We were staying in the same hotel, so it didn't take more than a few minutes to locate her room. I knocked and a moment later Charlie answered the door, wearing sweatpants and a t-shirt, with her hair tied up in a knot on top of her head. She looked like she was ready to hop into bed, and she was still the most beautiful woman I'd ever seen.

"Hey," she said with a small smile.

"Hey to you too." I gave her a peck on the cheek before she moved aside to let me in.

I don't know what came over me in that moment, but as soon as she locked the door and turned around, I slipped my arms around her waist and pulled her tight against me before my lips came crashing down onto hers. She seemed surprised by the sudden kiss, but a second later, she was melting into me and kissing me back.

Reluctantly, I pulled away after a few precious moments. "I'm so sorry about the other day. I should have never let you walk out that door." I brushed a stray lock of hair away from her face and tucked it behind her ear.

"I'm sorry, too," she said, looking down at her toes. "Of course, I want you to be there for Landon. I was being selfish—"

"Charlie," I put my finger under her chin and forced her to look at me. "You were not being selfish. I was being dumb. I was trying so hard to get you when we first met, that I forgot to keep that up once I had you. I should have known that just because your situation is different than Landon's, it doesn't mean you don't need someone there for you, too."

One corner of her mouth turned up into a brief smile as she nodded.

"I'm also pretty sure I mentioned at one point that I'm really bad at relationships," I added. "That's not an excuse, though. I take responsibility for what I said—or what I didn't say—and I promise to be there for you, listen to you, be a shoulder to cry on, whatever you need. I promise I'll be there, if you'll forgive me."

Before she said anything, she took a step closer to me, wrapped her arms around my neck, and nuzzled her nose against mine. "You're forgiven," she said.

Pressing my forehead against hers, I wrapped my arms around the small of her back, drawing her closer to me. "God, I love you."

I felt her body go rigid in my arms, and then she peeled her face away from mine. "You love me?" she whispered. Her eyes were soft, and the smile from before broadened ever so slightly.

The words had slipped out of my mouth without much thought, but now that I was thinking about it, I realized I meant it. I truly didn't think it was possible to fall in love with someone this fast, but it happened. I loved her.

I leaned forward and gave her a peck on the lips. "Yes, I love you, Charlie."

She bit her lip, and I guessed it was because she was trying to hide the huge, toothy grin on her face, but it didn't work. She smiled so wide, I was sure the corners of her mouth were touching her ears.

"Brody, I love you, too," she breathed.

Desire swept through my body, and I needed her like I needed air to breathe. I pulled her to me and kissed her. It was slow at first, but quickly turned into a deep, heated kiss where our tongues clashed together as we drew each other closer. She let out a small moan into my mouth, and that about did me in right then and there.

I worked my hands down to the hem of her shirt, and she lifted her arms as I gently pulled it up and over her head. Our mouths parted reluctantly so I could pull it away from her and fling it across the room. My eyes widened when I realized she wasn't wearing a bra, and she was now naked from the waist up.

"You're so beautiful." My eyes continued their sweep over her exposed skin, soaking up every detail. After a moment, she crossed her arms over her chest, and her shoulders sagged as if she were trying to hide.

I reached for her hands to stop her. "Don't do that. You're beautiful, and I want to see you."

She blushed and leaned in to kiss me again, this time much more tenderly. She pulled at my t-shirt, and soon, we were both topless as we continued to kiss each other passionately. She ran her fingers through my hair, tugging on the ends, while I slowly guided us towards the bed.

I felt like I had been waiting for this moment since I first laid eyes on this girl, and all my problems and worries began to melt away with each kiss we shared. I hardly remembered why I came here to talk to her in the first place.

When the backs of her legs hit the bed, I eased her down until she was lying flat and I was hovering above her.

She broke our kiss and met my gaze. I could see the fiery passion in her eyes, and I knew she wanted this as much as I did.

"Shit," I cursed and hung my head. "I don't have a condom." If I didn't stop now, I wouldn't be able to. Reluctantly, I went to stand up, but she took hold of my arms and held me in place.

"I'm on the pill," she assured me. "It's okay. Please." She placed a reassuring hand softly on my cheek, and I leaned into her palm before leaning down and taking possession of her mouth once more.

As much as I wanted to keep kissing her, I couldn't wait any longer. "Charlie, I need you." I pushed myself up and stood at the edge of the bed. With lightning speed, I kicked out of my shoes and went for the button of my jeans. Sticking my thumbs into my waistline, I slid both my pants and my boxers down my legs.

She didn't tear her eyes away from me the entire time I stripped, and I watched as her eyes lowered, soaking in every detail of my body. I let her admire me for a moment before reaching for the waistband of her sweatpants. She immediately sucked in a gulp of air and seemed to be holding her breath in anticipation. I waited, my eyes searching for her permission to continue. Instead of responding though, she placed her hands on mine and helped me wiggle her sweatpants down her legs. I added her clothes to my pile on the floor and allowed my gaze to sweep over her naked body.

"Come here," she whispered, holding her hand out to me.

"I just need to look at you for a second." I ran my hand through my hair and took my time admiring her. "I've been waiting for this since I first laid eyes on you."

Climbing onto the bed, I spread her knees apart and knelt between them. Placing my fingertips on her ankles, I smoothed my hands up her legs, feeling every inch of her skin. She trembled beneath my touch as my hands passed over her hips, her stomach, and finally rested on her breasts. They fit perfectly in my palms, and I began to massage her nipples with my thumbs. She arched her back in response, and I knew she was ready for me.

"Brody, I need you," she whimpered.

Keeping one hand on her chest, I braced my weight on the bed with the other as I leaned forward, and our mouths met once more. She wrapped her legs tightly around my waist, and she gasped when we became one. The way we fit together was as if we were made for each other. She fit me like a glove, and I never wanted this moment to end. I had never felt this way with any other woman I'd been with—and I doubted I *would* feel this way with anyone else. No one could measure up to her.

With every kiss and every move we made together, I felt myself growing both physically and mentally closer to Charlie, and I willed myself to last. This woman deserved all the pleasure in the world, and I planned on spending all night giving it to her.

******

It was nearly three in the morning, but Charlie and I were still lying naked together, talking and laughing about nothing in particular. She had her head rested on my chest, and her hand was splayed across my stomach.

"If your 100 back goes as well as your 200 back went, then you'll be heading to the Olympic trials with several races under your belt," I told her.

"Oh, my goodness!" She smiled. "I can't believe it. It really is a dream come true."

"You've worked hard, Charlie. Good things come to those who put the work in."

"That's true," she agreed.

She fell silent, and for a minute I thought she had fallen asleep. Lifting my head, I saw her staring at the far wall, presumably lost in thought.

"What are you thinking about?" I asked her.

"Well, I don't want to ruin the mood, but I've been waiting for you to bring up the stuff you had mentioned earlier about Landon and his dad."

I tried to stifle my groan. I hadn't brought it up because I had been distracted and totally forgot. As much as I wanted to fall asleep on a happy note, it was important to discuss this with her now.

She shifted her head so she was looking me in the eye. "We can talk about it tomorrow if it's too late."

Shaking my head, I turned onto my side so I could face her. "No, it's important to tell you now while we're alone."

She nodded and waited silently for me to continue.

"The other night, I went out to a bar after our fight."

She narrowed her eyes, and I realized I hadn't told her that.

"Nothing happened," I assured her. "I just wanted to get out of the house. I ran into Chase though, and he's the one who dunked my phone in beer, making it unusable for the rest of the night. Anyway, when I got home, Landon had let himself in with the spare key I gave him. He found something that raised some questions."

I explained to her the receipts Landon took from his dad's house, and how all the money had been taken from one account at Howard Enterprises. Upon some further investigation, we discovered it was indeed the account that had been robbed. I also told her Landon had discovered the money had been deposited in a foreign bank account under *his* name.

"What a monster!" Charlie covered her mouth in horror. "If he gets caught, wouldn't that mean they'd go after Landon?"

I nodded. "It looks like it. We have no idea why or how he's doing it, though."

"Oh, my God, the phone call from the other day," she gasped. "Allison and I overheard Mr. Davis at the office. He was talking to *Camila*. Do you think they could be working together?"

"Holy fuck." It did make sense. We overheard Camila at Howard Enterprises the day of the swim clinic. I found that gun in her room. Landon said he found guns in his dad's study. Camila would know how to transfer the money.

Charlie shook her head. "It doesn't make sense, though. Roman gives Camila anything she wants, why would she steal from him?"

156

"And why is she giving it to Mr. Davis?" I added. "I have no idea, but I think we need to keep an eye on those two."

"And do what? This could be dangerous, maybe we should just go to the police."

"No, not yet. Let me think about this for a while."

She turned to me, and her eyes shined with worry. "We don't know who else could be involved in this, and I don't think it's our business to get any more involved."

"Not our business?" I repeated. "Charlie, Landon's name is on those bank slips. Like you said, if they get caught, the police are going to go after him. I can't let that happen. We may have stumbled into this mess, but we're a part of it now."

She was silent for a long moment as she digested what I had said. Finally, she nodded slowly. "So, what do we do?"

I sighed. "I don't know yet."

She brought my hand to her lips and kissed my fingers. "I just don't want anyone to get hurt."

Placing each of my palms on either side of her face, I kissed her on the forehead. "No one is going to get hurt if I have any say in the matter. Now, let's try to get some sleep. There's not much we can do about it tonight."

She nodded again and nestled into my side. "I love you, Brody."

"I love you, too."

Chapter Nineteen

Charlie

When I woke up a few hours later, Brody was still sound asleep beside me. Faint snores escaped from his lips with the rise and fall of his chest. He looked so peaceful, and I hated that I would need to wake him up soon. Reaching forward, I gently massaged his cheek as I watched him sleep.

I loved this man. It sounded totally crazy, but it was true. We'd come such a long way in a short amount of time, and I couldn't wait to see what the future had in store for us. If it was anything like the last couple of weeks had been, it was going to be anything but boring.

Brody stirred beside me, and soon, his eyelids fluttered open. "Hey, beautiful." He smiled and stretched before he reached over and pulled me closer to him. "How long have you been awake?"

"Only a few minutes, I was about to wake you," I said, running my fingers along his jawline.

"Is that so?" He winked and flashed that devilish grin of his. "Ready for another round, are you?" He rolled over so he was on top of me, pinning me to the mattress.

I started laughing and held him at arm's length. "No, silly! We have warmups soon, and my parents should be here any minute. So, I hate to kick you out, but you need to leave."

"Ouch." He placed a hand on his chest and feigned disappointment. "Do I have to? We could just blow off the swim meet and stay here in bed all day." He started kissing my neck, and with each kiss, he moved further down my body.

He was nearly to my breasts before I finally stopped him. "Brody!" I giggled. "You keep this up, and I won't want to stop."

"That's the goal, babe." He sat up and winked.

"You can come back tonight, but right now, you need to leave before my parents see you in here."

"Alright, alright," he sighed. He stood from the bed and started pulling his clothes back on from the night before.

Wrapping the sheets around my naked body, I walked him to the door and kissed him goodbye.

"I expect you to be wearing this exact outfit when I come back tonight," Brody growled, running his hands along the bedsheet.

I just laughed and opened the door for him. He gave me one more kiss and was gone.

In record time, I threw on my clothes and gathered my things before my parents arrived a few minutes later to take off for the pool. When we arrived, we found that everyone else was already there, sitting in the same spot we had been in last night. To my surprise, Roman was also there, talking to Coach Tanner.

"Morning, Charlie." Allison smiled as she passed me on the stairs.

"Hey." I touched her shoulder to stop her. "What is he doing here?" I whispered, motioning to Roman.

She shrugged. "Sometimes they come to the meets. I'm assuming it's for photo opportunities or something. Makes them look good since they're sponsoring us."

"They?" I asked her.

"Yeah, Camila's around here somewhere, too." She chuckled when I rolled my eyes. "I'll be right back, need to get my suit on."

I waved to Landon, whose dad was nowhere to be seen, and smiled when I saw my parents were already deep in conversation with Allison's parents. I set my stuff down next to Brody, who was eating a breakfast sandwich and staring at me with a loving gaze.

"Long time, no see, Charlie." He winked.

I sat down next to him and gave him a playful shove on the shoulder. "Stop," I giggled. "I barely got dressed before my parents came to my room this morning."

"So, you're saying they almost got a free show?"

"You're impossible." I shook my head.

He laughed. "I'm only messing with you." He leaned in close and whispered in my ear, "In all seriousness though, I really had a great time with you last night." He gave me a small peck on the cheek and then stood to slide past me. "Going to go put my suit on."

I blushed as I watched him walk away.

Already dressed in my warmup suit, I decided I had enough time to go to the concessions stand and get a quick breakfast. That breakfast sandwich had made me hungry.

Once I had my sandwich in hand, I took a few bites as I made my way back to our spot in the bleachers. The hallway was quiet, as most athletes were either changing or hadn't arrived yet. I was enjoying the peace and quiet while I ate my breakfast—until I heard some shouting coming from one of the offices that lined the hallway. I was a little annoyed but didn't pay much attention to it, until I realized I recognized the voices.

I stopped in my tracks.

It was Camila and Mr. Davis.

Tiptoeing to the office they were in, I pressed my ear against the door to listen.

"I told you, I couldn't hack into the system this time," Camila said. "Unless one of your men are good with computers, we aren't getting through without bringing someone else in."

"We already have too many people who know what's going on," Mr. Davis' voice boomed through the wall. "I am not putting my ass further on the line for you. *You* got us into this mess. You're out of time."

"Oh, shit," I said under my breath. *They* are *working together.*

"No, please! Just give me another day." It sounded like Camila was begging. "I'll go back to Jacksonville now. I'll work through the night. I'll figure it out."

"You've had three weeks to get this done. What makes you think you can figure it out in twenty-four hours? No, we had a deal. We'll have to take care of Roman sooner than we planned. He's going to talk, and my men will be ready back home to do what needs to be done."

My eyes widened in horror.

"I never agreed to harm him," Camila said.

"Don't tell me you've actually developed feelings for the man?" Mr. Davis laughed.

"I didn't say that. But if we get caught, we'll be out the money *and* they'll know where to find us."

"News flash, sweetie: they already know where to find us. That's how this mess started. We've run out of options. We do this my way, now. We have ways to make him talk."

I suddenly felt a sneeze coming on, and desperately tried to hold it in.

Camila sighed. "Fine, you're right. What's the plan—"

"Ahchooo!"

Shit, not good. I couldn't hold it.

I heard footsteps on the other side of the door and knew I only had a few seconds before they'd find me. In two steps, I bounded to the other side of the hall where there was a bathroom. It was a men's bathroom, but I ducked inside anyway. I went to the first stall I saw and locked myself in it.

No one came into the bathroom behind me, but I couldn't hear anything outside either, so I couldn't be sure if they were still there or not. I didn't dare move.

After several minutes, it was still quiet, so I decided it was probably safe to leave. But just as I went to open the stall door, the bathroom door opened.

Great, now what was I going to do? I was in the men's *room.*

"That's weird," the mystery person said. "My girlfriend has those exact same flip-flops."

I let out a sigh of relief when I realized it was Brody. I ran out of the stall and into his arms.

"Thought those shoes looked familiar," he said, holding me close. "Care to explain why you're in the men's bathroom?"

"I had to hide." I tilted my head up so I could look him in the eye. "I overheard Camila and Mr. Davis talking. I was right, they are working together. They're going to do something to Roman tonight."

"What—"

"I don't know, but they said they're going to make him talk so they can break into his system again. Mr. Davis said something about needing money by the end of the weekend and not being able to wait any longer. They said they'll hurt Roman if they have to."

"Shit, you're sure?"

I nodded. "Yeah, I'm sure. What are we going to do?"

He ran one hand through his hair and shook his head in confusion. "I have no idea. Did you record the conversation?"

My shoulders sagged a little. "No, I don't have my phone on me."

"Don't beat yourself up," he reassured me. "We'll figure something out." He let go of me and started pacing back and forth. His forehead furrowed as he thought hard about what to do.

"Do you think the cops would believe us if we said anything?" I asked him. "Maybe the receipts would be enough to prove to them something bad is going on."

He shook his head. "We don't have time for that. Landon's name is on them, remember? They'd have to do an investigation before they would arrest his dad. I think our only option is to catch them in the act."

I choked back a laugh. "You're not serious, are you?"

"I'm dead serious. We don't have time to think of another plan. We need to find Landon and catch him up."

"So, we're really going to do this?" I asked, a bad feeling settling in my gut.

He nodded. "Yeah, we're going to do this."

******

We told Landon what I had overheard, and even though he was a little hesitant, he agreed to help us follow his dad tonight. We agreed that we would all take turns staying close to Mr. Davis, Camila, and Roman throughout the rest of the day to see if we could overhear any plans they may have. It was risky, and possibly wouldn't provide any information, but it was the only option we had.

In the meantime, we went about the meet as we otherwise would have. We swam all our races, and other than sneaking off to spy on the suspects every now and again, we behaved as if we were at any other swim meet.

Standing by the starter's table, I was now waiting for them to call my heat to the blocks. This was my final race of the day—the 100 backstroke finals. The rest of my swims had gone well, but this was my best race, and I was excited to see how it would go. I won the prelims round earlier today and was confident I could do it again tonight. Another first-place win under my belt would make me so incredibly happy and proud of all the hard work I put into the sport all these years.

When the event before mine had exited the pool, the officials lined us up behind our respective blocks, and I knew it would only be moments before my race started.

"Hey, Charlie!" A shrill voice sounded from behind me.

My stomach dropped when I realized who it was. "Camila, what are you doing? I don't think you're supposed to be on deck."

162

"Oh, you're funny," she laughed and gave me a playful punch on the shoulder. "I'm giving your timer a bathroom break. Told him I'd fill in." She beamed at me with way too much enthusiasm.

If possible, I was pretty sure my stomach dropped even further. "Do you even know what you're doing? I—"

"Don't be ridiculous," she interrupted. "Now, get ready for your race."

I wanted to argue further, but she was right, I needed to focus. I took a moment to clear my head of everything that had nothing to do with the race—including Camila. I blew out a long, slow breath, and took a couple of arm swings to loosen up and shake away the nerves. Pressing my goggles tightly around my eyes, I was ready and waiting for the whistle. When I heard it, I jumped into my lane and situated myself on the wall as I clung to the block. I let out one final breath as I tried to relax.

"Take your mark!" the official shouted.

A split second later, the buzzer sounded, and I flew from the wall. A few short, powerful, dolphin kicks later and I broke the surface and started pumping my arms as fast as they would go. The more swings I took, the stronger I felt. Out of the corner of my eye, I could see the bodies of the other swimmers slowly falling behind as I took the lead. This only fueled me to go faster.

Within seconds, I was at the halfway mark. I pushed off the wall and once again used my strong dolphin kicks to widen the distance between the other swimmers and myself. As I continued to slice through the water, I noticed the fatigue I usually felt at this point wasn't there.

I could go faster.

Kicking it up a few more notches, I gave the last 20 meters of the race everything I had, plus some. Only when I finished into the wall did the exhaustion finally catch up to me, and I sucked in a huge gulp of air to catch my breath.

I lifted my goggles from my face, and my eyes darted to the scoreboard. Searching for my time, I was confused when it didn't appear on the screen. My gaze shifted over to Coach Tanner, who also appeared to be confused. He looked to me, then at the scoreboard, and back to me again. His brows furrowed and he started marching over to a nearby official when my time still hadn't come up.

I turned to Camilla to see what happened, but as soon as I saw her, I knew.

She stood above me with the timing pickle in her hand, and once our eyes met, she finally pressed the button. "Oops," she said, glaring at me. "I guess I didn't know what I was doing after all."

My mouth dropped open when I realized she had deliberately sabotaged my race. I should have won, and she took that away from me. Normally, I would have shaken hands with the other ladies in the lanes next to me, but I was so angry, I immediately pulled myself out of the water instead.

"What the hell are you playing at?" I growled at her.

She held her palms up, feigning innocence. "Come on now, Charlie, accidents happen."

"Bullshit!" I got right up in her face. "You did that on purpose."

"So, what if I did?" She shrugged. "What are you going to do about it?"

"Why would you do that? What did I do to you?"

"You were listening in on a private conversation!" she hissed, her voice getting low. "I saw you duck into the men's restroom, and you're fucking lucky it was me who saw you, and not Davis. This is your only warning to mind your own business. Next time I catch you sticking your nose where it doesn't belong, the consequences will be much more severe."

Before I could say anything more, Coach Tanner appeared at my side with the head official. "Camila?" he said when he reached us. "*You* were timing?" He turned back to the official. "Bruce, you let her time? She just sabotaged my swimmer's race!"

"Now, hold on, Tanner," the official—Bruce—said, attempting to reason with Coach Tanner. "We don't know it was Camila's fault. There could have been an issue with the timing pad."

"No, it was Camila!" I piped in. "I saw her push the button long after I had finished the race. She did it on purpose."

"Charlie," Camila gasped, clutching her hand to her chest. "That is an awful big accusation, don't you think?"

"It is a big accusation, young lady." Bruce crossed his arms and arched his brow at me. "Even if Camila made the mistake, we can't say she did it on purpose."

"Bruce, for God's sake, my swimmer should have won that race!" Coach Tanner's face was turning a deep shade of red. "You saw it."

Bruce held his hands up. "Luckily, the timing system has a backup time for situations such as this. It won't be exact, but it'll be close."

"It could be enough to cost her the win," Coach argued.

"Tanner!" Bruce snapped. "That's enough. You know there isn't a lot to be done in this kind of situation. My hands are tied." He walked off to resume his duties.

"Sorry," Camila chirped, before she also turned and walked away.

I clenched my fists at my side and resisted going after her. Coach Tanner put his arm around my shoulders and guided me in the opposite direction.

"We'll just wait and see what the backup time comes out as. Trust me, I'm just as frustrated about this as you are."

Somehow, I doubted that, but I didn't argue.

When we returned to the rest of the team in the stands, they immediately descended upon me with questions of what happened.

"What the hell was that about?" my dad demanded. "Anyone with eyes could see you won that race!"

"Camila was timing my lane," I grumbled.

"I don't know what that means," he said. "Who's Camila?"

"That's a bunch of bullshit," Allison added. "How was she allowed down there?"

I wanted to bitch and complain about it, but it wasn't going to help anything, so I simply shrugged.

My mom scooped me into a hug and held me tight. "Charlie, sweetie, I know this isn't fair. We'll get through this. Maybe it'll still work out in your favor."

I nodded, but I wasn't sure if that would happen or not. Looking over her shoulder, I saw Brody was standing behind her, two steps up. His brows were furrowed with concern, and his eyes were filled with sadness. I broke away from my mom and went to hug him next. Wrapping my arms tight around him, I buried my face in his neck.

He kissed me gently on the cheek. "I'm so sorry, Charlie," he whispered. "What can I do to make you feel better?"

I pulled back enough so I could look him in the eye. "You can help me expose that bitch and get her the hell out of my life."

Chapter Twenty

Brody

"I know where they're going," Landon said as I opened my hotel room door to let him in. He came rushing by me so fast, I didn't have a chance to register his words right away.

"Where?" Charlie asked, immediately standing from her chair. She had arrived a few minutes ago, and we were waiting for Landon to get there to figure out the game plan.

"I overheard him talking on the phone. He thought I was napping. They're going to the abandoned Pullman Yard, it used to be an agricultural machine factory. It's not far, and he left right before I came over here. They're probably almost there." His words fell out of his mouth a mile a minute and my head started to spin.

That didn't leave us with a lot of time to figure out a plan.

"What do we do now?" Charlie's face turned white as she looked to me for direction.

I gulped. "I guess we're going to the Pullman Yard."

We didn't waste any time as we sprinted down to the lobby and hailed a cab. Thankfully, it was a Saturday night in a big city, and it didn't take us more than a minute or two to track one down. The three of us piled in and told the driver that we were in a hurry. He simply nodded his head and didn't ask any questions. He didn't even say anything when we asked to be dropped off a few blocks away. I pulled a wad of cash out of my pocket and gave him a big tip.

Once he was gone, we quickly made our way to the abandoned building, trying to remain as quiet as possible. It was dark outside, so the chances of being seen were slim, but we stayed low to the ground just in case.

"There's my dad's rental car," Landon whispered, pointing to a black Cadillac SUV parked near the building.

We tiptoed up to what used to be a window but was now just a big hole in the side of the building, overgrown with nature. We peered over the edge to look inside, and even though it was dark, someone had lit a small fire in the middle of the room so we could see what was going on inside. I noticed Roman first, who was tied

166

up to a chair a few feet away from the fire. Camila and Mr. Davis stood off to his right, having a conversation I couldn't hear. A fourth person paced the floor directly behind Roman, but I didn't recognize him.

"That's the guy that was at my dad's house the other day," Landon whispered, reading my thoughts. "Victor, I think his name was."

"So, what do we do now?" Charlie said, lowering herself below the open hole in the wall. Both she and Landon looked at me expectantly.

"Do you have your phone on you?" I asked Landon.

He nodded, pulling it out of his pocket.

"Call the cops. Tell them where we are and what's going on, and then get off the phone as quickly as you can. We don't want to make more noise than necessary. Charlie, you go around that side of the building and see if you can get close enough to hear them without being seen. I'll do the same on this side."

"Shouldn't we wait for the cops?" she asked.

I shook my head. "A lot can happen before they get here. If I can help save someone from getting hurt or killed, I'm going to do what I can. I understand if you don't feel the same. You can stay with Landon if you'd prefer."

"No, I'll go." Her voice quivered, and she was visibly trembling.

"Hey." I placed my hand on her cheek, forcing her to look up at me. "We're going to be fine. Okay?"

She nodded, and I quickly kissed her before we each took off in either direction. Landon stayed put, dialing 911 as I turned the corner of the building.

Shuffling along the side of the building, I crouched down next to an opening in the wall that was about twenty feet from where Camila and Mr. Davis stood. Roman sat surprisingly calm as he glared at the two of them. Victor was still pacing behind him, and even though I suspected he would have some kind of weapon on him, my heart still skipped a beat at the sight of the gun in his right hand.

I redirected my focus back to Mr. Davis, who appeared to be speaking with someone on the phone, while Camila was standing beside him attempting to catch bits and pieces of their conversation. A moment later, he hung up, and the two of them turned to face Roman.

"Roman, this is the last time I'm going to ask nicely," Mr. Davis' deep voice growled. "Either tell us how to get into the system so we can get to the account, or we will have to force it out of you."

"I'm not telling you anything," Roman spat.

"Roman, dear, please—"

"Shut the fuck up!" He roared, making Camila jump. "I should have known you were behind this. After everything I did for you, this is how you're going to repay me?"

Before Camila could respond, a loud crash, as if someone had fallen on a pile of debris, came from the other side of the building.

Exactly where I suspected Charlie was.

"Is someone there?" Mr. Davis yelled, his voice echoing throughout the old building. "Show yourself!"

I prayed Charlie was okay and that she would stay put.

"You," Mr. Davis pointed to Victor. "Go see if someone is there."

Victor started sauntering over to the other side, his gun aimed and ready to shoot. I couldn't stand the thought of them finding her, so I did the only thing I could think of to distract them.

"I'm over here," I said, entering the building through the hole in the wall. I stood still with my fists clenched at my sides, as all four of the people in the room turned towards me at once.

"Brody?" Camila said, her voice full of shock. "What the hell are you doing here?"

"I'm here to stop this."

"HA! How exactly do you plan on doing that?" Mr. Davis chuckled, shaking his head. "It doesn't matter. Victor, finish him."

Victor turned from where he was standing and shot the gun in my direction. I was able to dodge the bullet, and with adrenaline coursing through my body, launched myself towards him. I was nearly on top of him before he shot again. This time, his bullet struck my shoulder, knocking me to the ground.

I clutched my arm as the blinding pain took over. The pain was so strong, I thought for sure I would pass out any moment. Victor stood above me with the gun pointed at my head, and I squeezed my eyes shut as I prepared to die. Instead of a gunshot though, I heard a bone-crunching smack, followed by a thud. I opened my eyes to see Victor lying unconscious beside me, and above him, Charlie stood with a large piece of plywood in her hands.

"Charlie," I breathed, relieved that she was okay.

She stared in horror as she realized what she had done. The piece of plywood in her hands dropped to the floor with a crash, and she froze to her spot.

"Finish them both!" Mr. Davis roared. Both he and Camila shot forward, Mr. Davis towards Roman, and Camila towards Charlie.

"Charlie, look out!" I attempted to get in between Camila and Charlie, but the pain in my shoulder was too great, and I couldn't move fast enough.

A moment later, Camila took Charlie down to the ground, and she was pinned beneath her. Charlie struggled by swinging her arms and kicking her feet, but Camila delivered a solid punch to Charlie's chin, and the blow stunned her long enough that Camila was able to get her hands around Charlie's throat.

"Charlie!" I screamed and fought through the pain to get on my feet.

My gaze went to Mr. Davis, who had untied Roman just enough so that he could pick him up off the chair and throw him over his shoulder. He turned and took off for the far end of the building where we had left Landon. I was tempted to go after him, but Charlie needed my help.

Camila still had her hands around Charlie's throat, and Charlie was gasping for air while she struggled beneath Camila. If I didn't act quickly, Charlie could die. I took a step towards them and stepped on something hard.

Victor's gun.

Picking it up, I knew what I had to do. If I hesitated for even a moment, I wasn't sure I'd be able to go through with it. Aiming the gun, I pulled the trigger, and the bullet hit Camila square in the head. A moment later, her lifeless body flopped to the ground on top of Charlie.

Charlie sucked in a huge gulp of air as she struggled to get her breath back. Now that I knew she was okay, I turned in the direction that Mr. Davis had taken off with Roman. He was nearly to the exit, when suddenly Landon jumped out from behind the wall and blocked his way.

"Move, boy!" Mr. Davis' voice boomed. Given his track record with his son, I knew he wouldn't have a problem plowing right through him to get away.

I took a deep breath and willed myself to ignore the pain in my shoulder long enough to run after them. I could hear police sirens getting closer to us now, and knew we only had a few minutes before they would be here.

"Landon!" I yelled to him. "Catch!" I threw the gun at him and he caught it effortlessly.

He held it towards his father, who came to a halt a few steps away from him. "Stop, or I'll shoot!" Landon shouted.

"You don't have the balls to shoot me." Mr. Davis laughed and proceeded more slowly towards Landon.

"Landon!" I yelled again, urging him to do *something*.

He hesitated for only a single moment, and then he aimed the gun lower and shot his father in the foot. Mr. Davis screamed in pain and dropped Roman from his shoulder as he fell to the ground, clutching his foot.

Landon froze with the gun still pointing at his dad. His eyes were saucers, and he was breathing so hard and fast, I thought he was going to hyperventilate. I rushed to his side and took the gun from him.

"You did good, Landon," I assured him. "You did good."

Less than a minute later, the cops had arrived on the scene and were rushing towards us with their guns drawn. I dropped Victor's gun to the ground away from Mr. Davis and put my good arm above my head. There were at least a dozen officers and they had us surrounded.

"Which one of you called 911?" One of them shouted.

"I did," Landon said, taking a cautious step forward. He pointed towards Mr. Davis on the ground. "This is my father. He was attempting to force information out of the man lying next to him."

"He had two helpers," I interjected. "Those two over there." I pointed to the other side of the building, where Victor still laid unconscious, and Camila's body was sprawled out in a pool of her own blood. Charlie was now on her feet, standing next to Camila's body with her arms above her head. Blood was splattered across her face and the front of her shirt.

"Get these men in handcuffs," the police officer ordered, pointing to Mr. Davis and Victor. "And check for a pulse on the woman. The rest of you, stay put. The paramedics will be here shortly to address your injuries. We'll be needing to ask you some questions."

******

The paramedics arrived a few minutes after the officers did, and immediately tended to the injured. One of the ambulances took Mr. Davis away to be treated for his gunshot wound, and a police officer went with them to make sure he wouldn't try to escape. Victor had regained consciousness and was sent off in another ambulance to check for a concussion. A police officer went with him as well.

I was also transported to the hospital to have my gunshot wound treated. The last of the adrenaline from this evening wore off at some point during the ride over there, and I was in so much pain I could barely think of anything else. Fortunately, the paramedics pumped me full of pain meds, and the pain had dulled slightly by the time I arrived at the hospital.

They rushed me to the emergency room, and a young male doctor immediately began tending to the wound. I was probably there a full ten minutes before they decided I needed to be taken into surgery. However, surgery prep was a bit of a blur, as I was pretty high on pain meds and not entirely sure what was going on around me.

All I remembered was a blur of people dressed in white, rushing around me and saying things I couldn't make out. I had tried asking where they were taking me, but couldn't tell if words were actually coming from my mouth. Then there was a bright light before everything went dark.

Sometime later, my eyes fluttered open, and I was in a small hospital room, connected to a dozen wires, and sore as hell. Peering through my eyelids, I could see Charlie seated on the end of the bed. My heart dropped when I saw the black and blue marks around her throat and on her chin.

She turned towards me as if she felt me watching her, and I saw her eyes widen and her smile light up. "You're awake!" she shrieked, as she moved closer to my side. "How are you feeling?

Do you remember anything? We've all been worried sick about you." She pointed to Landon, Allison, and Coach Tanner, who were also gathered around the room.

"Charlie, let the man wake up," Coach Tanner chuckled softly. "I'm going to get the nurse."

"How long have I been out?" I asked, as Landon and Allison also gathered around my bed.

"It's been a couple of hours since they brought you in for surgery," Charlie said. "Landon and I had to stay behind for questioning, but as soon as they let us go, we called Coach Tanner and Allison and we came straight here."

"I knew something had to be wrong if I was getting a call from Coach Tanner after midnight," Allison said. She placed a hand on my good arm. "It was really brave what you did, Brody. Stupid. But brave."

I chuckled and then winced from the pain in my shoulder. "Thanks, Allison."

A moment later, Coach Tanner re-entered the room with a nurse following shortly behind him. She was a short woman dressed in purple scrubs, with greying hair pinned to the top of her head. Her face lit up when she saw I was awake, and she approached my bed with a wide smile.

"Brody, I'm glad to see you're up," she said sweetly. "I'm Wendy, I'm the nurse who's been tending to you. Do you mind if I check your vitals really quick?"

I nodded and she went to work. She asked me several questions on how I was feeling while she checked my blood pressure and changed my bandages.

"It sounds like you were really lucky, Brody," she said while she was taking my temperature. "The surgeon said the bullet didn't go all the way through, and it didn't hit any vital organs. You'll be sore for a while, obviously, but other than some PT, you should have a smooth recovery." She checked on all the wires I was hooked up to, replaced a bag of fluids, and pushed some buttons on the machine before she turned her attention back to me. "Everything looks as good as can be expected at this point, Brody. I'll let the doctor know you're awake, and he will come to chat with you soon."

I thanked her as she left the room, and then turned my attention back to Charlie and the others. "So, what else happened after they took me away?"

Charlie glanced at the others before she turned back to me. "Camila was pronounced dead," she said.

"I see." I waited for the guilt to hit, but to my surprise, I didn't feel anything. Did that make me a monster? She was a big part of my life at one point. But she was also trying to kill Charlie, which I wasn't going to let happen. If one of them had to die, I was glad it wasn't her.

"It was self-defense, man," Landon said from across the room. "They're not going to charge you with anything. If you hadn't done anything, Charlie would have died instead."

"I know." I reached for Charlie's hand and gave it a hard squeeze when she took it. "Would you guys mind if I have a few minutes alone with Charlie?" I asked the others.

"That's fine," Coach Tanner said, standing up from his chair. "Landon, let's go get some flights rounded up. I'm sending you three home today. You're in no shape to be finishing this meet. Allison, if you'd like to go get some rest, I'll call you a cab."

"Thanks, Coach, but I'll stay," Allison said. She turned to me, "We'll be back in a few minutes."

The three of them left the room, leaving Charlie and me alone. She got up and laid down next to me on the bed, resting her head on my good shoulder.

"Charlie, I'm so sorry—"

"Shh." She cut me off. "Don't be sorry. You saved my life. I'll take a few bumps and bruises if it means I still get to live to see another day."

"You saved my life too," I told her. "If you hadn't taken out Victor, he would have killed me."

"I know, but I don't want to think about what would have happened if I hadn't gotten there in time." She shuddered next to me. "By the way, you shouldn't have sacrificed yourself like that. I was ready for him."

"I wasn't going to let anything happen to you." I turned and kissed her on the forehead. "I got us into this mess, I wasn't going to let you get hurt."

"I think we were all equally in this mess long before last night. I don't want to point fingers though. It's done, we're all going to be okay. That's that."

"What about Landon though?" I sighed. "His father is most likely going to jail. And I wouldn't want Landon living with him after this anyway."

"Landon has us. He's going to be eighteen in a few months, and then he can legally be on his own. He's going to be fine."

"What about my swimming career?" My breathing picked up a notch as the thought entered my mind. "I'm not going to be able to swim for a while—"

"Brody." She placed her fingers over my mouth and propped herself up on one elbow so that she was looking down at me. "Relax. Okay? Yes, you are going to have to take some time out of the water to heal, but it won't be that long. You'll be able to get back to swimming, and you'll be great. It's just a little setback. It's not the end of your career."

I closed my eyes and attempted to take some slow, calming breaths. "You're right." I opened my eyes and placed a hand on her cheek to pull her in for a kiss. "Thanks for keeping me level-headed. I love you."

She smiled and kissed me again. "I love you too."

A knock at the door interrupted us, and I looked up to see Coach Tanner standing in the doorway. "I'm sorry, Charlie. Is it alright if I have a word with Brody?"

She nodded and stood from the bed. "Absolutely. I'll be right outside." She turned and shot me a small smile before leaving the room.

Coach Tanner pulled up a chair next to my bed and took a seat. He leaned forward on his elbows and blew out a heavy sigh. "How are you feeling?" he asked after a long pause.

"I've felt better," I said. "But I'm not in as much pain as I was before."

He shook his head. "What were you thinking? Not only did you put yourself in danger, but Charlie and Landon could have been hurt—or even killed. I just want to know what all of you were thinking."

"I didn't make them come with me, Coach, they chose to—"

"Of course, they chose to come with you!" he exclaimed. "Landon looks up to you. He goes wherever you go. You really think he'd let you put yourself in danger alone? And I'm not blind, I've seen the way you and Charlie have been getting along. She's in love with you. She'd do anything for you, too."

I laid there in silence and stared at the ceiling as I thought of a way to respond. He was right, they would have come with me even if I had begged them not to.

"I shouldn't have put us in that situation," I finally said. "But I knew something was going on, and I had to do something. We had evidence, but it was complicated, and we ran out of time. I didn't know what else to do."

Coach Tanner nodded slowly as if he was absorbing the information. "I'm not going to lie, Brody. It was admirable what you did. You probably did save that man's life and his company. I am sorry about what happened with Camila. If you want to talk about that—"

"I don't."

He nodded again. "I understand." He reached out and gave my arm a reassuring pat. "I'm proud of you, Brody, but please don't ever put yourself or my other swimmers in this kind of situation again. Do you understand?"

"Yes, sir," I said.

"You know you guys are like family to me. I don't know what I'd do if I were to lose you. I care more about your safety than anything else, and that includes swimming. Am I upset that you won't be able to compete for a while? Of course. This is your career, I get how important it is. But I would so much rather you be alive and healthy and not swimming, than gone for good. I care about you guys too much."

"Thanks, Coach. You're like family to me, too. I would never do something to upset you, unless there was good reason for it. I felt like this was a good reason."

"It was. But now it's done, and we're going to move forward. We'll figure out what to do with you while your arm heals when we get home. I got you all on a flight out of here at ten AM. As long as your doctor clears you, that is."

As if he knew we were talking about him, the surgeon who had operated on my arm knocked on the door and entered a moment

175

later. "Brody, I'm glad you're awake. Let's take a look-see, shall we?"

Chapter Twenty-One

Charlie

Brody was discharged from the hospital early Sunday morning, and then he, Landon, and I left for Jacksonville. When we landed, we all went to Brody's house to watch the rest of the swim meet and cheer Allison on from afar. Even though she hadn't gotten much sleep the night before, she did phenomenally and placed top three in all her races.

Coach Tanner decided to give all of us Monday off to recover from the crazy weekend, so the three of us decided to spend the day at Brody's. We slept in, and we had just finished eating a late breakfast when Brody offered to wash the dishes.

"Hold on," Landon said, taken aback. "Who are you, and what have you done with Brody Hayes?"

"Ha. Ha. Very funny." Brody rolled his eyes and began clearing dirty dishes from the sink with his good arm so he could fill it with water. "I'm tired of living in filth. I'm going to spend some time cleaning today."

"Was a near-death experience all it took to get you to start cleaning?" I poked fun at him as I brought my plate to the sink.

"If y'all are going to make jokes, you can make yourself useful and help," Brody shot back, chuckling.

Landon started laughing. "I guess I could pitch in. I'd hate to see how long it takes to clean this place with one good arm." He went to the living room and began picking up dirty dishes from the end tables.

I gave Brody a quick kiss on the cheek and went to find a vacuum.

An hour or so later, the dishes were clean, the floors were mostly vacuumed, and the placed was starting to look much better. I was in Brody's utility closet, looking for more cleaning supplies when there was a knock at the door.

"I'll see who it is," I said, heading for the door. When I peeked through the peephole and saw who was standing on the other side, my mouth dropped open.

"Who is it, babe?" Brody called across the room.

I turned towards the boys. "It's Roman. He's alone."

Brody appeared wide-eyed around the corner. "What do you think he wants?"

"I don't know." I shrugged. "Do I let him in?"

"Yes, let the man in," Landon urged.

I opened the door slowly, and Landon appeared by my side before anyone said anything.

"Hi," Roman said quietly. "I hope I'm not interrupting anything. Can I come in?"

Landon and I both looked to Brody for his permission, and he nodded.

"Sure." I moved aside to allow him in. "Can I get you something to drink?"

He shook his head. "No, no, that won't be necessary. I wanted to talk to the three of you about what happened the other day. Is it alright if I sit?"

"Yes, please do." I motioned for him to take a seat at the kitchen table, and the rest of us followed suit.

Roman waited until we were all settled before he spoke. "Well, I don't want to waste anyone's time. I'll get straight to the point. First of all, I want to thank each of you. Not only did you save my company from losing a ton of money—again—but you probably saved my life. I'm not sure what they would have done to me, but I'm sure it wouldn't have ended well for me." He cleared his throat and shifted in his seat.

"I also want to apologize to you, Brody," he continued. "I should have believed you when you told me how terrible Camila was. The whole time I thought you were acting out because you still had feelings for her, and you were jealous. But now I understand. If she did even half of what she did to me, to you, I can totally understand why you felt the need to total my car so many weeks ago."

"Sir," Brody spoke up. "Not sure it matters now, but I was also telling the truth when I said my friend was the one who smashed your car, not me."

Roman sighed and combed a hand through his hair. "I'm sorry, I should have listened to you. That would have saved us a lot of trouble, I think."

Silence fell over the room, and Brody, Landon, and I all exchanged a look while we waited for Roman to continue. When it was clear he wasn't going to, I spoke up.

"Roman, if you don't mind me asking. Why did you stay with Camila for so long? You had to have noticed her selfish tendencies in the amount of time you were with her."

"Oh, trust me, I did," he chuckled. "Honestly, I don't know if I have a good answer for that. I knew she could be a very terrible person, but at the same time, she had a way of making you feel special. I realize now it may have all been an act, but at the time, it felt real. And of course, I always knew there was a possibility she was only with me for my money, but I didn't want to admit that to myself because I cared about her. Maybe I was hoping I would bring out the good in her. I don't know."

"I get it," Brody said. "I was with her for a long time, too. She had a way of saying the right things and doing whatever it took to get her way. I'm only glad it didn't take me very long to see through her act."

"You seemed to know her much better than I ever did." Roman looked down at the ground when he spoke. "I should have known what she was up to. She was living under my roof for God's sake."

"Roman, I wouldn't continue to beat yourself up over it," Brody said. "She was much smarter than I ever gave her credit for. We may never know the true depths of her deception."

"That's what scares me. I just wish I knew what her motive for it all was."

"Well, she's gone now," Landon assured him. "We don't have to worry about it anymore."

Roman continued to stare at the ground as he slowly nodded his head. His eyes were wide and unblinking as if he were lost in another world. The three of us remained silent as we allowed him to process everything that was said.

Finally, after what felt like several minutes, but what was probably only a few seconds, Roman blinked rapidly and looked up at us once more. "So, Brody, how long are you out of the water for?"

Brody seemed relieved for a change in subject, even if it was about his injured arm. "Out of the water completely for the next eight weeks. After that I can slowly ease my way back into it."

"Are you going to need additional funds while you recover?" Roman asked. "It's the least I can do given everything that's happened. Plus, I'm supposed to be getting the stolen funds back in a few days. Would $200,000 be enough to cover your finances for a while?" He took a checkbook out of the inside pocket of his jacket and flipped it open to a blank check.

Brody, Landon, and I stared at each other in shock as we realized he was seriously going to write a check for $200,000 like it was no big deal.

"Roman." Brody put his hand on top of the checkbook to stop him. "I appreciate it, but I don't need your money. I've picked up some more sponsors since the story broke. I'm going to be just fine financially."

Roman shook his head and looked completely flustered as he put the checkbook back in his pocket. "There has to be *something* I can do to repay you. Money is the best thing I can offer. Unless you wanted a job? I could offer you a job—"

"You don't owe me, or any of us, anything," Brody interrupted him. "We were more than happy to help take care of the situation."

"I don't know if *happy* is the word I would use," Landon mumbled. Brody gave him a quick jab in the side, and he fell silent again.

"Roman, if you really want to thank us, you can continue to sponsor our team and get us to our meets," I said. "Continue to do exactly what you are doing for us."

"I can do more than that." Roman nodded. "I can get more involved. Get you more equipment. Set up more camps—"

I put my hand up to stop him. "I think what you are doing now is more than enough."

Obviously, I didn't know Roman as well as Brody and Landon, but I knew Brody was often annoyed with how involved Roman got as a sponsor. I didn't need him to double his involvement and drive everyone crazy.

"I agree with Charlie." Brody nodded. "Just keep doing what you're doing."

He threw his hands up in defeat. "Alright, I can do that. But please let me know if you change your mind. I owe you all my life."

Brody stood up and shook Roman's hand with his good arm. "We'll let you know, Roman. We appreciate it."

******

Later that evening—long after Roman had gone home—we were done cleaning for the day and were planted in front of the TV in Brody's living room. I had ordered pizza for us for dinner, and we ate in silence while we watched the Marlins game. Brody and I were snuggled up on the couch, with my head laying on his good shoulder and my arm splayed over his belly. Landon sat across the room from us in the recliner, gently rocking back and forth. When the eighth inning ended, and a commercial came on the TV, Landon stood from his chair.

"I think I'm going to go to bed." He stretched his arms above his head and turned to leave the room. "Don't forget I've got that meeting at the courthouse in the morning, so I won't be at practice."

"Sounds good, man," Brody said. "What time is it at? I'm going to go with you."

Landon stopped in his tracks. "Why?"

"Because I want to be there for you. I've put you through enough shit. It's the least I can do."

The smallest hint of a smile danced on his lips. "It starts at eight."

"Great. Be ready to go at 7:30. We'll head over then."

Landon stood at the bottom of the stairs a moment longer, staring down at his hands as he rubbed them together, seemingly thinking of what to say. "Brody?" he finally said.

Brody tore his gaze away from the TV once more. "What's up?"

"Thank you." He gave Brody a lopsided smile, then turned and went upstairs.

"Do you really think they're going to let him legally stay with you until he turns eighteen?" I asked Brody when I heard Landon's door close. When he didn't answer right away, I lifted my head to make sure he had heard me. "Brody?"

He was staring in the direction of the TV again, but his eyes were glazed over as if he was lost in thought. When he felt my stare, he shrugged his shoulders and shook his head. "I don't know, but I'd rather he stay here than get sent off to some family he doesn't even know. Especially since he turns eighteen in only a few months. I'd really like it if he could keep his life as normal as possible until *he* can decide what he'll do next."

I nodded. "I hope he can stay here, too."

181

"I'd really like it if you stayed here with me as well," Brody said.

"I'll stay here as often as you want me to." I snuggled into him further, resting my head back on his shoulder.

He put his hand under my chin and forced me to look back up at him. "No, I want you to *stay* with me, Charlie. I want you to live here."

My mouth dropped open and I sat up straight to look at him. "What?"

"I want you to move in with me," he repeated.

"Brody, we haven't been together very long. Are you sure that's a good idea?"

He nodded. "Yes, I'm very sure. Charlie, I'm in love with you. I'm not going anywhere, and I want you here with me."

"What if it doesn't work out?" I asked.

"Do you think it won't work out?"

I thought about it before I answered him. Honestly, I had never felt like this with someone before—not even Nick. And we had been through *a lot* together in the short time I'd known him. I really could see a future with him. Maybe we were meant to be together.

I smiled down at him. "I think it'll work out."

"So, is that a yes?" He smiled back.

"It's a yes," I giggled.

He pulled me close to him and kissed me like he'd never kissed me before. I clung to him, afraid if I let go, I'd wake up and realize this was a dream. His hand slid slowly down my back and rested on my butt. He gave it a hard squeeze and I couldn't stop the gasp that escaped from my lips.

"I need to get you upstairs," he breathed in between kisses.

I giggled and reluctantly broke the kiss. "Maybe you should take it easy. You did just have shoulder surgery."

He groaned and dropped his head back in disappointment. "I hate that you're right."

I laughed, "Get used to it, buddy. It happens a lot."

He smiled, and then his face got serious as he ran his thumb over one of the bruises Camila had given me. "I'm never going to let someone hurt you like this again."

Leaning my face into his hand, I turned my head to kiss his fingers. "Let's go to bed. We have an early morning."

Slipping out of his grasp, I stood from the couch. I held out a hand to help him up, and he wrapped his good arm around my waist as we climbed the stairs. Once we were in bed and under the covers, he leaned over and gave me another kiss.

"You know, as much as I want to help Landon with everything going on, I do wish I could swim with you and Allison in the morning," he whispered.

I turned onto my side, so I was facing him, and brushed some hair out of his eyes. "I know. Remember, this is temporary. You'll be back at it and breaking records in no time."

He smiled and closed his eyes. "I love you."

"I love you, too."

Within minutes, I could tell he had fallen asleep. I continued to smooth his hair back soothingly as I watched him dream.

As I lay there, I couldn't help but think about how happy I was. My life was falling into place, and even though there were a few speed bumps thrown in, everything felt right in this moment. I had a feeling a life with Brody was going to be anything but boring, and I couldn't wait to find out.

Epilogue

Mr. Davis

"Davis, you have a visitor."

My cell door swung open and in walked Officer Rios, the young, over-attentive correctional officer that came to get me every time I was allowed to leave this bloody hellhole.

"I don't want to see anyone. I have a headache." I slumped in my wheelchair in the corner of the cell. I had been staring at the wall for the last few hours—it was actually how I'd spent most of my time here—trying to figure out how the hell I was going to get out of here and pay back the money we owed.

"You always have a headache." Officer Rios smirked and came behind me to push my wheelchair out of the cell. "It'll do you some good to talk to someone. How's the foot feeling?"

"It would feel better if you gave me some alcohol or something to numb the pain," I grumbled.

"Can't do that, man," he chuckled as if it were a joke.

I crossed my arms and glared straight ahead as he pushed me out and down the hallway towards the visitor center. It was surprisingly quiet in there, only one other inmate had a visitor this afternoon. Officer Rios pushed me past him, went all the way to the end, and parked the wheelchair at the last window.

My stomach dropped when I saw who was there to see me. How did she know where I was?

"I'll leave you to it, Davis." Officer Rios patted me on the shoulders like we were good buddies and walked away.

I was too shocked with who sat before me to be annoyed.

Bringing the phone to my ear, I swallowed before I spoke. "What are you doing here?"

"Why do you think?" she spat back.

"Listen, I don't have the money—"

"I know you don't have the money," she hissed. "And I know Camila is dead!"

"That wasn't my fault—"

"We'll discuss that later." Her face was bright red with anger. "I don't have a lot of time, so listen carefully. He knows you're here, and he knows Camila is dead. That doesn't excuse the fact that you owe him a lot of money. He's more pissed off than ever."

"What am I supposed to do?"

"Shut up and let me finish." Her eyes shot daggers my way. "I'm going to help you get out of here, and help you hide out until it's safe. I can help you get the money."

I shook my head in confusion. "Why would you do that?"

She sat back in her chair and smirked. "Because I want revenge on that bastard who killed Camila. And you're going to help me get to him."

\### \#

Continue reading with *Sink or Swim Vol. 2*, available soon!

Please visit my website to view my weekly blog – and don't forget to sign up for my mailing list for exciting updates and offers! https://meganreiffenberger.com/

Also, join me on Facebook: https://www.facebook.com/SwimmingThroughLyfe. I love to hear feedback from my readers!

If you enjoyed *Sink or Swim Vol.1*, please consider leaving a review! Reviews are critical for other readers to discover my books.

Thanks for reading!!

Megan Reiffenberger

Author Bio

Megan Reiffenberger was born in 1994 in Watertown, South Dakota, and has lived there most of her life. She graduated from George Mason University with a Bachelor's Degree in Marketing, and she currently works at Lake Area Technical College, as the Student Activities Coordinator. If she's not working or writing, you can often find her going for a run or a swim, as regular exercise is of the utmost importance to her. In fact, inspiration for Megan's first novel, *Sink or Swim,* was drawn from her sixteen years of competitive swimming experience.

If you want to know more about Megan, or when her next book comes out, please visit her website at https://meganreiffenberger.com/ or follow her on Facebook (Swimming Through Life), Twitter (@Megan_Reiff22), and Instagram (reiffenberger22).

Made in the USA
Middletown, DE
17 February 2022

61439518R00106